W9-BCM-701

Matchmaking rule #1:
don't get caught up in your prospects.
Even if they are gorgeous and charming.

"I watched you stare at Grant when he walked away." Phoebe drilled Molly with her all-seeing gaze. "You were interested all right."

"I was interested because my matchmaker radar went off when I met him," Molly said.

Phoebe frowned. "Because...you wanted to fix him up with me?"

"Yep. That's what I do, Phoebs."

"You know I'm not looking for romance," Phoebe said.

"Maybe this time it would be different."

"I doubt it. You of all people should know that."

Molly agreed with Phoebe. She'd always dreamed of falling in love, but she'd given up on romance. Safer that way. "Things change. Maybe it's time."

"You can say whatever you want, but you're the one who'll be seeing him again, not me," Phoebe said.

A little frisson of excitement squiggled through Molly at the thought of seeing Grant again, taking her a bit off guard. She'd need to watch those reactions. Rule number one couldn't be ignored. Ever.

Books by Lissa Manley

Love Inspired

*Family to the Rescue
*Mistletoe Matchmaker

*Moonlight Cove

LISSA MANLEY

decided she wanted to be a published author at the ripe old age of twelve. She read her first romance novel as a teenager when a neighbor gave her a box of old books, and she quickly decided romance was her favorite genre, although she still enjoys digging in to a good medical thriller.

When her youngest was still in diapers, Lissa needed a break from strollers and runny noses, so she sat down and started crafting a romance, and she has been writing ever since. Nine years later she sold her first book, fulfilling her childhood dream. She feels blessed to be able to write what she loves, and intends to be writing until her fingers quit working, or she runs out of heartwarming stories to tell. She's betting the fingers will go first.

Lissa lives in the beautiful city of Portland, Oregon, with her wonderful husband of twenty-seven years, a grown daughter and college-aged son, and two bossy poodles who rule the house and get away with it. When she's not writing, she enjoys reading, crafting, bargain hunting, cooking and decorating. She loves hearing from her readers and can be reached through her website, www.lissamanley.com, or through Love Inspired Books.

Mistletoe Matchmaker
Lissa Manley

Love Inspired

If you purchased this book without a cover you should be aware that this book is stolen property. It was reported as "unsold and destroyed" to the publisher, and neither the author nor the publisher has received any payment for this "stripped book."

Recycling programs for this product may not exist in your area.

™ LOVE INSPIRED BOOKS

ISBN-13: 978-0-373-81593-7

MISTLETOE MATCHMAKER

Copyright © 2011 by Melissa A. Manley

All rights reserved. Except for use in any review, the reproduction or utilization of this work in whole or in part in any form by any electronic, mechanical or other means, now known or hereafter invented, including xerography, photocopying and recording, or in any information storage or retrieval system, is forbidden without the written permission of the editorial office, Love Inspired Books, 233 Broadway, New York, NY 10279 U.S.A.

This is a work of fiction. Names, characters, places and incidents are either the product of the author's imagination or are used fictitiously, and any resemblance to actual persons, living or dead, business establishments, events or locales is entirely coincidental.

This edition published by arrangement with Love Inspired Books.

® and TM are trademarks of Love Inspired Books, used under license. Trademarks indicated with ® are registered in the United States Patent and Trademark Office, the Canadian Trade Marks Office and in other countries.

www.LoveInspiredBooks.com

Printed in U.S.A.

Let all bitterness and wrath and anger and clamor and slander be put away from you, with all malice: and be kind to one another, tenderhearted, forgiving one another, as God forgave you.
—*Ephesians* 4:31–32

This book is dedicated to my longtime critique partners, Terri Reed and Leah Vale. As always, thanks, guys, for helping me finally get this book right! I really couldn't have done it without you.

Chapter One

"Stop that dog!"

The words were barely out of Grant Roderick's mouth before he realized they were futile. Nothing was going to stop the streak of white fluff running down the Christmas-bedecked boardwalk of Main Street in Moonlight Cove, Washington.

Crazy mutt. Fast, too. Fast, and sneaky enough to have bolted by him when he'd opened the front door of his aunt's house to get the mail.

Grant followed Jade, his aunt's white standard poodle—the one he was supposed to be taking care of—running like a madman trying to keep up with the runaway dog. Thankfully, the dog looked smart enough to keep out of the street and away from cars. If anything happened to Jade, he'd never forgive himself.

Grant dodged a holiday shopper coming out of one of the many quaint stores lining the street.

"'Scuse me," he said, straining his neck to keep an eye on Jade. If he lost sight of the dog, he'd never get a hold of her. How could he have let the crazy canine get the better of him one measly day into his house/dog-sitting duty?

All of a sudden, Jade stopped so fast she almost left paw skid marks. Yes! A block behind, Grant kept running, hoping she stayed put so he could grab her. He had work to do, work that didn't involve chasing naughty dogs all over town.

He drew closer, and Jade put her large, furry paws onto the Christmas-light-festooned window of a store and let out a hearty *woof.* Then she dropped to all fours again. Grant kept moving, closing the distance between them, pretty much expecting her to take off when he got within grabbing distance. She was clever, he'd give her that. She'd outsmarted him. For a while.

But she stayed by the store, her white pom-pom tail wagging up a storm. Just as she reared up on her hind legs again and pawed the air with her front paws, he was in striking distance.

I've got you now!

He lunged for her collar...and saw the store door open to his left. As quick as a cat—for a large dog—Jade jumped forward and through the open door. She looked like she was smiling as she dodged past him.

He fell forward, unable to stop his momentum,

and crashed to the thankfully dry boardwalk with a bone-jarring thud. The air whooshed out of him instantly, and he couldn't draw a breath to save his life.

He rolled onto his back, cringing, wondering if anything was broken. He lay there for a moment, flopped out like a dead fish.

Just as he managed to choke some air in, a feminine voice exclaimed, "Oh, my goodness, are you all right?"

He looked up and saw a very pretty woman with a mass of long curly red hair and cute freckles staring down at him, her eyebrows drawn together over a set of gorgeous green eyes.

His cheeks burned. Great. He'd fallen down in front of the most attractive woman he'd seen in a long time. All he could do was groan, his pain mingling with complete embarrassment.

Not exactly a stellar way to start his time in Moonlight Cove, was it?

Molly Kent looked down at the blond man lying on the sidewalk in front of her store, Bow Wow Boutique, concern rippling through her. He'd hit the deck pretty hard.

Given that he was chasing Jade, Molly surmised this guy had to be her friend Rose Latham's nephew, Grant Roderick, whom Rose had enlisted to pet-sit Jade while she went on a Hawaiian honeymoon with her new husband and former neighbor, Benny Fulton.

"I'm fine," the man said from between clenched teeth. With a grimace that told Molly he wasn't all that fine, he got his feet underneath him and stood.

Peter and Parker, her two schnauzers, barked from within the store, clearly excited by Jade's arrival, as well as, Molly supposed, the commotion outside. Their bell-trimmed Christmas collars jingled with every yip.

"Are you sure?" She reached out a hand but stopped short of touching him when she got a look at him dead-on. Her breath snagged. Never in her wildest imaginings had she expected Rose's nephew, whom the older woman had described as a socially backward computer jockey with a serious need to get out more, to be so attractive. He was tall, had nicely chiseled features and a strong, shadowed jaw. Cute. Very cute.

He nodded, his face slightly red, giving her a crooked smile, then spread his well-muscled arms wide. "Luckily, I'm pretty tough." The short-sleeved navy blue polo shirt he wore emphasized that he was in serious shape—and that he hadn't left the house prepared for the chilly December weather.

"You must be Grant," she said, feeling her face heat a teensy bit. If she didn't know better, she'd think he made his living in front of a camera rather than behind a computer.

"Right," he said. "I suppose chasing Jade gave me away."

"I saw you through the window." She held out a hand. "I'm Molly Kent."

He shook her hand, his grasp strong. And undeniably warm. "Nice to meet you, Molly Kent."

He looked right at her, and she couldn't help but notice his eyes were a really compelling blue. She tried not to stare.

Feeling a bit off-kilter from his killer good looks, she fell back on manners and familiar territory. "Now that Jade is contained, would you like something to drink? I have a fridge in the back." Molly had promised Rose she would look after Grant and Jade while Rose was gone, and Molly never reneged on a promise. Besides, being needed felt good.

"Sorry," he said. "I have work to do."

Molly raised a brow and looked at Jade as she panted in between drinks from the water bowl Molly kept out for Peter and Parker, and any other dogs who visited. "Jade needs a rest," she said pointedly. "And you look like maybe you do, too."

"Yeah, I guess maybe I do," he admitted. "Even though it's cold out, I ran all the way here and really got my blood flowing." He glanced at Jade, who, Molly noted, was now chasing Peter and

Parker around one of the pet food displays, having turned their attention from Grant and Molly to each other. All three dogs barked in delight as they ran in a wide circle, around and around and around.

He shook his head. "She's clever and fast. I'm a runner, and even I couldn't keep up with her."

She chuckled, then gestured him in, her eyes on the rambunctious canine trio. "Especially when she's motivated to find her way here for lots of doggy fun. As you can see, they all love to play."

"And pull off successful escapes." Grant grimaced as he followed her in, closing the door behind him. "I'm pretty sure she was waiting for me to open the door so she could take off."

Molly laughed as she navigated her way around the Christmas squeaky-toy display. "You're probably right. Jade is a handful. Even Rose and Benny have a hard time curbing her wandering tendencies."

Grant trailed behind her. "I guess I don't feel so bad then, for letting my guard down long enough for her to escape."

Molly reached the back room. "No, you shouldn't. Jade is kind of high maintenance, especially if she misses playtime." She opened the mini-refrigerator on the right, pulled out a bottle of water and handed it to him. She jumped a bit when their fingers touched. Whoa.

She cleared her throat. "Just a hint, but a played-out dog is a contented dog, and will want to be your constant companion." She paused for effect. "Did you remember playtime?"

He furrowed his brow as he twisted open the water bottle's top. "Oh, yeah…playtime." He shook his head, then drank some water. "I forgot."

She'd thought so. "Well, again, don't worry. If she escapes again, Jade always comes to visit me and my two dogs, so I can just bring her back."

"Okay," he replied, rubbing his eyes. "I've never owned a dog. This is all new to me." He turned and looked at the mangled bright yellow remnant of what had to be a tennis ball Jade dropped on the floor behind him. "Do they all have such… disgusting toys?"

Molly smiled. So, he was clueless about dogs, something she found surprisingly endearing. Good thing she was the resident dog expert around Moonlight Cove. She had a lot to teach him. "Pretty much. My two schnauzers each have four or five tennis balls rolling around, and they're all pretty slobbery."

"And smelly," he replied, making a face. "Maybe I should buy her a new, clean one."

Molly appreciated his suggestion. He caught on fast. "Well, you could, but it'll be gross, too, pretty quickly, won't it?"

He smiled. "I guess so. Maybe I need an endless supply."

Molly's heart rate kicked up a notch at his gorgeous smile—including dimples—and the way his eyes crinkled at the corners.

She forced her thoughts back to the conversation at hand, wishing her heart rate would slow down a teensy bit. "The Sports Shack sells them. I'd give you one, but Jade likes the ones fresh out of the can." She remembered something. "Hey, I'm guessing you can get a family discount since Kim is married to the Sports Shack's owner, Seth."

Seth and Grant's cousin, Kim, had met five months ago when she and her seven-year-old son had come to Moonlight Cove to live with her and Grant's aunt Rose. Seth had saved Kim from drowning in a riptide off Moonlight Cove Beach, and Kim had ended up working in his store. Soon after, they fell in love, and the rest was history.

"Good point. I met Seth when he, Kim and Dylan came to visit me in August."

A thought occurred to Molly. "You weren't at their wedding, though, were you?" The happy bride and groom had been married this past September in a lovely ceremony at Moonlight Cove Community Church, followed by a reception on the beach where they'd met.

Grant shook his head. "No, I couldn't make it."

"For your cousin's wedding?" Kind of an important event to miss....

His jaw tightened, and he seemed to be squirming. "I was out of the country for work."

Molly nodded. Seemed as if Grant was a workaholic. Remembered pain shot through Molly. Her father had missed her high school graduation because of work, too. Never again.

Shoving aside past hurts, she said, "Well, since you missed the nuptials, I'm happy to report that Seth and Kim are very happy, and completely devoted to each other and Dylan." Truth be told, Molly kind of envied the love they shared and the family they'd built, though she knew that kind of love wasn't in the cards for her. From now on, she would only let God into her heart—she could depend on Him to never let her down.

"Good to know," Grant said evenly.

"My friend Phoebe told me they went to Seattle."

"Yeah. Seth had some kind of Mariners function for former players."

Seth had played for the Seattle Mariners for three years before coming back home to Moonlight Cove to take over running the Sports Shack from his father.

"Did they kennel Cleo?" Molly asked. "I hope not. I would have been glad to keep her."

Jade had had a litter of pups in June, and Rose

and Benny had given Cleo, one of Jade's puppies, to Dylan soon after Kim and Seth got engaged.

Grant shook his head. "Nah, they took her with them. Rose told me Dylan just about had a hissy fit when they talked about leaving her here."

"Not surprising. Dylan and Cleo come in here all the time to play with Peter and Parker and to pick out toys. He's pretty attached to her." She made a face. "But I'm not sure I'd want to take her on vacation."

"Why not?"

"She's even wilder than Jade," Molly said, quirking a brow.

He looked horrified. "Is that possible?" he asked, glancing sideways at Jade. She was still madly chasing the jingling Peter and Parker in circles around the predominantly green and red displays, their toenails clickety-clacking on the dog-practical linoleum floor. "She seems pretty wild to me."

"You think *this* is wild?" she asked, gesturing with her head toward Jade. "Wait till you meet Cleo."

He took a swig of water, then returned her smile, his eyes sparkling. "I'm not sure I want to," he said, clearly joking.

She stared at him for a moment, really liking his sense of humor. Then she caught herself and dragged her gaze away. "Listen," she said, moving around him and out into the middle of the store, next to the leash display, where there was more space. "If you want me to pick up some tennis balls for Jade after work, I'd be happy to drop them off later."

He raised his blond brows. "No, that's fine. I don't want to put you out."

"Oh, you wouldn't be putting me out. I need to pick up some fishing lures for my elderly neighbor from the Sports Shack, anyway. Floyd broke his leg and still wants to go on a fishing trip, wheelchair and all, with one of his buddies. I promised when I checked on him last night to deliver some lures later today."

"Well…that'd be great." Grant glanced quickly at his sporty-looking watch, then frowned slightly. "Oh, wow. Look at the time. Tick-tock. I really should get back to work."

"Tight deadline?"

"Extremely tight," he replied, rubbing his jaw. "I have to have this job done by January 1 for initial system testing, and then the rest completed by the middle of January, which is an insane deadline for this kind of a product. So that means I have days and days of nothing but work ahead of me."

She had visions of him working day and night, alone and isolated, his job his only focus.

Sounded sadly familiar. Would Grant someday be like her dad, all alone, because he chose work over everything else? She hoped not. Her dad had ended up pretty unhappy, with no one. Molly couldn't think of anything worse.

Thankfully, she had her large group of friends to keep her company. And God, of course.

Molly hadn't grown up going to church, but ever since she'd come to Moonlight Cove, she'd found great comfort and sense of family at the Moonlight Cove Community Church.

"I'm happy to help out," she told Grant. "Your aunt asked me to look in on you and Jade. She said you get all tied up in work and forget to take breaks to eat." She smiled. Although, she had to admit, he didn't look particularly underfed. A guy didn't get enough muscles to stretch a T-shirt just right by not eating well.

Molly blushed at her train of thought.

He lifted his strong chin and peered at her from under incredibly long lashes. "My aunt asked you to check up on me?"

"Kind of, but not in a bad way. Rose just thought you might need some help." She pointedly looked at Jade, who was now flopped on her back, her paws in the air, wrestling with Peter and Parker. "You said yourself you don't have any experience with dogs."

He chuckled, then held his hands up in the air like the dog, the light in his eyes dancing. My, he was handsome. "Touché. I'm clueless," he reminded her.

"Not exactly clueless," she replied, heading toward the front counter. "Just inexperienced."

She leaned over the counter and picked up a gift-wrapped sample package of the chicken liver dog treats she had on display next to the register. "Here's my tip. Keep some of these with you at all times. Jade will never leave your side." She handed the treats to him. "I know for a fact she loves them."

He took the package, looking dubious. "You sure?"

The sound of twelve paws skittering on the floor echoed through the store.

"I'm sure," she replied with a wry twist of her lips as she nodded to the three dogs who now sat obediently at his heels. "They're giving you their best 'we're starving to death' looks right now."

He glanced down at the supposedly starving dogs.

"Now you know my big secret," she said with mock-seriousness. "With those treats, you'll be the Dog Whisperer in no time. Take those, on the house."

"Thanks," Grant said, tucking the small pouch of treats in his back pants pocket. "I'll be sure and keep these handy."

"Glad to help," Molly replied truthfully.

Grant cast his gaze around. "Um...do you by chance have a leash I could borrow? Now that I've got Jade under control, I don't think I want to let her loose again."

"Sure thing." Molly headed to the front of the store and grabbed one of her own leashes from a hook by the door. She held it out for Grant. "Here you go. I'll just get it back when I deliver the tennis balls."

Grant walked over and took the leash, his blunt fingers brushing Molly's again. "Thanks."

Her breathing hiccupped.

"I really appreciate your help. Obviously, I need it," he said, his gaze as warm as a sun-splashed Caribbean ocean.

She stared at him for a moment, then pried her gaze away, trying not to lose herself in his stunning eyes. "It's the least I can do for Rose and Benny." Never mind a nice guy who was handsome and charming to boot.

All three dogs came belatedly running when they caught sight of the leash, clearly making the connection between it and the possibility of a walk.

"Sure you don't want to take all three?" Molly asked brightly, her tone teasing. "You've got treats and a leash. Doesn't get any better when you're a dog."

Grant considered Peter, Parker and Jade, who

were now excitedly dancing the cha-cha around his feet. "No sirree," he replied, wagging his head. "I can barely handle one. Three...? No way am I ready for that."

"Don't tell me you're scared of a few mutts," she said mischievously, enjoying her and Grant's flirting...um, *banter.*

He gave her a serious look. "Hey, I almost lost my aunt's beloved pet, and the crazy dog managed to make me fall on my face in front of a pretty lady. You bet I'm scared."

She felt a flush of pleasure. He thought she was pretty? "Don't be," she managed. "As long as you establish yourself as the pack leader, you'll be good."

"Pack. Leader." He flexed like a he-man body builder. "Got it."

Molly giggled unabashedly at his antics. Add sense of humor to the list of his attractive traits. Not that she was paying attention. At least not for herself. But as the town's matchmaker, she was always keeping an eye out for eligible singles.

"I've got to head home," Grant said, holding up the leash. "Any tips for getting this thing on?"

She nodded toward the chicken liver treats in his back pocket. "Hold up one of those, ask her to sit and hook 'er up. Should be easy."

"Whatever you say." Grant took the treats out of his pocket, ripped the Christmas wrap off and fished a few from the bag. He faced the dancing bevy of dogs and asked Jade to sit in a firm, deep voice that resonated in Molly.

All three dogs sat.

"What do you know?" Grant said, giving each one of them a treat.

Molly squatted and held on to Jade just as Grant leaned down to hook the leash to Jade's collar. His face came close, and she got a whiff of his aftershave, all spicy and clean, and another look, up close and personal, at his impossibly long eyelashes framing his eyes.

She fought the crazy urge to run her fingers over those lashes. Instead, she concentrated on the inane detail of the curly texture of Jade's nose fur.

Grant hesitated, just a few inches away, seemingly concentrating on hooking the leash onto the ring on Jade's bright pink collar.

Molly chastised herself for being so drawn to him, so caught up in the details of everything about him. What was wrong with her, anyway?

He got the leash attached, and he straightened.

Molly let herself draw a breath, realizing she'd been holding it.

"That was easy," he said. "Thanks again for your help. I think I've got the hang of this dog stuff now."

"Great. You're a fast learner." Good. No, bad... he wouldn't need her around now.

Thrown off balance by her weird thoughts, Molly focused on instructing him how to give the standard poodle another treat, complete with "Good dog, Jade." She fell back on the familiar to keep herself on an even keel and to counteract her attraction to him. She had to get herself together.

He was Rose's nephew. Not some guy she wanted to date. Well...she'd kind of like to date him, but wouldn't. Too much danger down that trail.

The buzzer on the front door sounded, heralding the arrival of a customer. Molly looked over and saw her friend Phoebe Sellers walk in, right on schedule for their lunch date.

Her *single* friend....

Instantly, Molly's trusty matchmaker hat figuratively popped onto her head. She quirked a brow as she realized that Phoebe might be Grant's perfect match.

Making a mental note to strategize about setting them up, she headed toward Phoebe. "Come on over and meet Phoebe," she said to Grant. Might as well see if sparks flew.

Even little sparkles would help tell the story. Fortunately, it didn't take much for Molly to sense who belonged with whom. Some said she had a gift for recognizing perfect matches, and with eight successful ones in the last two years, she'd have to agree.

"Phoebe, this is Grant Roderick, Rose's nephew." Molly turned to Grant. "Grant, this is Phoebe Sellers. She owns the ice cream store up the street."

Grant extended his hand and smiled. "Nice to meet you."

"It's mutual," Phoebe said as she shook his hand, a decidedly speculative gleam in her blue eyes.

Oooh. Gleamy eyes. Always a good sign.

"How long have you owned the ice cream place?" Grant asked.

His interest in Phoebe had Molly's rapt attention.

"About a year and a half," Phoebe said, unwinding her fluffy black scarf from around her neck. "But I was born and raised in Moonlight Cove."

"Ah, a local girl," Grant said. "Looks like you've put down roots. You must like it here."

Aha. Mention of roots. Wonderful.

"I love it," Phoebe replied. "How long will you be staying?"

Interest, or just politeness? Phoebe had sworn off romance, too, but minds could be changed if need be. Maybe.

"Aunt Rose and Benny will be back just before

New Year's Eve," Grant said. "So I'll be around for a while."

"Well, it's good to have a new face around here." Phoebe smiled. "Small towns tend to get a bit boring."

Molly watched the whole exchange with interest, taking mental notes. No giant sparks yet, but it was early. And the gleam in Phoebe's eyes and Grant's questions…well, it could bode fairly well for a tidy setup.

Anticipation sparked; Molly couldn't wait to sink her chops into a good matchmaking prospect. She delighted in helping others find the true love she would never have; if she couldn't have a soul mate, well, then at least she could be a part of helping others find that special someone. It would be the closest she'd ever get to a happily ever after.

She pushed away the sadness that thought caused and tuned back to the matchmaking opportunity at hand. True love was elusive, and it took skill to make good matches that lasted; she'd have to pay attention.

"You two want to hang around awhile and just…talk?" Molly asked.

Grant held up Jade's leash. "Sorry, I can't. I need to get going." He gave a mock-salute. "Ladies, it's been a pleasure."

Phoebe murmured her goodbye in unison with

Molly, and Grant left, Jade trotting obediently at his side, her tail held high.

Molly watched him go. Nice guy. Very appealing.

If she were looking for a friendly, charming, all-work-and-no-play kind of guy. Which she definitely wasn't. At least not for herself. But Phoebe? Now, that was a different story.

Molly turned around to find her blonde friend standing right behind her, her arms crossed over her chest.

"He's very cute," Phoebe said, one brow arched.

Good sign. Physical attraction definitely played a part in who was meant to be together. Not the whole part, of course, but an important piece for sure.

"You think so?" Molly asked, careful to hide her matchmaker's eagerness by looking at a tiny green-and-red cable-knit dog sweater.

"Definitely attractive," she said, sounding amused.

Molly looked up at Phoebe. Her friend had her lips curved into a smile that definitely held a sly edge. "Maybe he's available," Phoebe said.

Molly peered at her friend more closely, her stomach flipping in a half circle. What was with Phoebe's wily grin? "For who?" she asked, hoping her suspicions weren't true.

"For *you,* of course," Phoebe said, shrugging.

Molly's tummy flipped all the way around. "For me?" She waved a finger in the air. "I'm not interested in him." Which was true. Except as a match for Phoebe. Or anyone who wasn't Molly. Rule number one of matchmaking: don't let yourself get caught up in your prospects. Even if they were drop-dead gorgeous and charming to boot.

Phoebe snorted. "Oh, right. I saw you getting all flustered when he bent down to hook the leash. I watched you stare at him when he walked away." Phoebe drilled Molly with her all-seeing, sky blue gaze. "You were interested, all right."

Trust Phoebe to catch the details. She was one of the most observant people Molly knew.

Molly put the sweater in its place and headed to the register, telling herself she shouldn't be surprised by Phoebe's statement. It was no secret she thought Molly should be dating, even though Phoebe wasn't dating, either. She'd lost her fiancé, Justin, God bless his soul, in a firefighting accident one and a half years ago, and hadn't dated since.

Time to set the record straight. "I was interested in him because my matchmaker radar went off when I met him."

Phoebe frowned, pausing, then moved closer. "Because…you wanted to fix him up with *me?*"

"Yup." No use hiding the truth. "That's what I do, Phoebs."

"You know I'm not looking for a romance," Phoebe said.

"Maybe this time it would be different."

"I doubt it. You of all people should know that."

Molly straightened some paperwork on the counter. She actually agreed with Phoebe about romance and its pitfalls. Molly was a romantic idealist at heart, and had always dreamed of falling in love, having a family and living a faith-based life. But since Jeff had dumped her three years ago—after Carl had dumped her a year before that—she'd given up on romance. Safer that way.

"Things change," Molly said softly. "Maybe it's time."

Phoebe paused and drew in a heavy breath, pain shadowing her eyes. "My situation's different than yours," she said.

Molly reached out and squeezed her arm. "Yes, it is, no doubt about it. What you went through when you lost Justin was awful, and much worse than what I went through. But do you really want to be alone forever?"

"Do you?" Phoebe asked pointedly.

Molly flushed. Trust Phoebe to turn this dating thing around by deflecting the tough questions back to Molly. But she'd asked an excellent question, one that heralded an impasse.

But not a surrender.

So she said, "I'm not sure." Best to at least appear to leave her own possibilities open. No sense in reinforcing Phoebe's love phobia with talk of her own. That would be counterproductive.

Phoebe rolled her blue eyes. "You can say whatever you want, but you're the one who'll be seeing him again, not me," Phoebe said.

A little frisson of excitement squiggled through Molly at the thought of seeing Grant again, taking her a bit off guard.

She'd need to watch those reactions. Carefully. Rule number one couldn't be ignored. Ever.

She leveled an amazingly droll gaze on Phoebe. "I will see him again, because Rose asked me to look in on him once in a while. But that's all, trust me." Molly would make sure of it.

"Really?" Phoebe asked, pulling her wild blond hair back with the elastic band she kept around her wrist. "'Cause I'm pretty sure I saw a spark."

Molly silently admitted Phoebe was right. Molly did find Grant attractive, and she'd been sparking all over the place. And boy, did she need to put a lid on the fire. She wasn't looking for a romance, especially with a man who seemed to be a workaholic like her dad. She would just admire Grant from afar, while keeping her promise to Rose.

Molly found her purse and pulled out her wallet to pay Phoebe for lunch. "Really," she replied, doing a good job of sounding detached. Now she just needed to follow through and act the part so she could do her matchmaker thing and find a way to get Phoebe and Grant out on a date.

Phoebe shot her a look coated in doubt—despite her grief over losing Justin, she remained a pure romantic at heart when it came to other people—so Molly changed the subject to the reason Phoebe was here—lunch.

"So, what are we having for lunch today?" Molly needed to stay at the store, since her one employee, Gena, had the day off. She and Phoebe were going to share some kind of takeout in the back room.

"I'm craving deli. How does a ham sandwich from Elly's sound?"

"Perfect," Molly said, glad Phoebe had dropped the subject of Grant.

Molly needed to do the same. Pronto.

No matter what, she had to ignore Grant's gorgeous blue eyes, beautiful smile and charming ways. She believed in finding everlasting, real love.

For everyone…but herself.

Chapter Two

After Grant left Bow Wow Boutique, Jade obediently trotting beside him thanks to the treats in his pocket, he went home and dug into his work. Somehow he managed to focus on computer code rather than on the appealing Molly Kent.

Sure, he'd noticed how pretty her gold-flecked green eyes were when he'd bent close to put on Jade's leash. And how smooth and creamy her skin was, with a light dusting of freckles across her pert nose. She was friendly, too, and had a good sense of humor to round out the package quite nicely. But the fact remained, he was here to meet his deadline, not resurrect his social life, which was nonexistent for a reason.

Work and romance just didn't mix, as his ex-girlfriend Jenna had proved to him when she'd broken up with him in grad school. How ironic was it that she'd dumped him for almost flunking out because he'd paid too much attention to her?

No doubt about it. Being successful and having a romantic relationship were mutually exclusive. Not something he was going to forget anytime soon. And he sure wasn't going to make the same mistake again. Not even with someone as attractive as Molly.

Turning his thoughts away from the past and how it affected the present, he noted that, thankfully, Jade seemed pooped by her visit with Molly's dogs. She'd plopped down on her bed in the corner when they'd come home, and had pretty much left him in peace to work for the better part of the afternoon. So he lost himself in his complicated task, only occasionally distracted by visions of Molly's pretty eyes dancing through his brain.

Sometime later, the burn in his shoulders forced his attention away from work. He rose and massaged the kinks that were trying to take up permanent residence in his upper back. While he rolled his shoulders and stretched, he looked out the big picture window running the length of the front of the house.

The green-gray Pacific Ocean spread out in all its beauty for as far as he could see. White-capped waves rolled in to the shore, and seagulls dipped and soared here and there. The clouds had broken up a bit, and the sun was actually peeking through, sending golden beams of light into the roiling ocean. Wow. What a view.

Man, his mom would have been all over this.

A shaft of grief pierced him, literally taking his breath away. He pressed a hand to his heart, trying to breathe.

His mom had adored the beach, and they'd often spent time here with Aunt Rose while he'd been growing up. But Mom was gone now, and he'd never share another walk on the beach with her again. Or another breathtaking scene like the one before him.

His eyes burned.

With practiced determination, Grant shoved his grief down into its cage where he wouldn't have to deal with it. Instead, he reiterated in his mind how important his job was to him, focusing on his career goals rather than his grief.

He'd come a long way from being the brainy geek with the pen protector in his pocket who everyone had laughed at in high school. Only at church had he been accepted. He'd found solace, community and appreciation there, and he'd truly found a connection to the Lord.

But then God betrayed him by taking Mom. And suddenly, Grant's faith had been shattered.

Now, he was so close to finally cementing in stone the lasting career respect he needed. Work was the only thing that mattered. He sat down and got back to his computer code.

Sometime later, a knock sounded on the front

door, jerking Grant from his work-induced haze. Jade sounded the bark alarm.

Grant looked up, his eyes burning, just in time to see her sprint to the door.

He rose from the makeshift computer station he'd set up at the antique roll-top desk in Aunt Rose's living room and glanced at his watch. Six-thirty. Wow. Where had the afternoon gone?

Stretching the kinks from his back and shoulders again—maybe a few aspirin would do him some good—he headed to the front of the house.

Jade was waiting by the front door, her tail wagging, obviously eager to greet their visitor, whom, if he guessed right, had long curly red hair and stunning green eyes.

Molly.

His heart rate kicked up a notch, but he ignored the sensation. She was just here to deliver tennis balls for Jade, right? Nothing to get all excited about.

He opened the door, holding Jade's collar—he learned fast—and saw Molly standing on the other side of the door, her face wreathed in a pretty smile that did funny things to his insides.

"Hi!" she said, her voice bright and sunny, which was all the sunshine he'd get today, given the cloudy skies. She held up a blue bag in her left hand. "I stopped at the Sports Shack and brought Jade some fresh tennis balls."

He couldn't help but smile back; her good mood was infectious after a long day of dry programming. "I figured it was you," he replied, pulling a squirming Jade back, putting his shoulders into the task. Boy, the dog was strong, and obviously wanted to get to Molly.

"Remember the treats?" Molly asked, nodding to Jade, who was about to pull his arm out of its socket. "Better use them now."

"Oh. Yeah." Grant felt his back pocket with his free hand, then pulled the treats out.

"Tell her to sit, and stay," Molly instructed. "Use a firm but kind voice."

"Sit," he said firmly. "Stay."

Jade instantly sat, her coal black eyes beaming up at him.

"Now, give her a treat and praise her," Molly said.

He dug a treat out of the bag and hastily gave Jade one. "Good dog."

She gobbled it up and kept her gaze homed in on him.

Grant turned to look at Molly, shaking his head. "Amazing. It works every time."

She shrugged. "What can I say? Most dogs will do anything for food."

He tucked the treats back into his pocket. "Gotta remember that."

She held up a bag of groceries in her other hand. "Speaking of food, I brought stuff to make spaghetti."

He blinked. "I really shouldn't take any time away from work," he automatically said. Though, actually, a break sounded great.

Molly peered around him, her gaze landing on his already well-used work area. "Looks like you've been at it for a while."

"Yeah." He swiped a hand over his face. "Pretty much all day."

"Maybe you could use a breather."

His thoughts exactly. He hated to admit it, but she was probably right.

"Everyone needs to eat, don't they?" she asked when he didn't respond. "Doesn't spaghetti sound good?"

His stomach growled. "I don't want to impose." Although, a home-cooked meal was sounding better and better. He'd eaten a quick breakfast of toast and eggs early this morning, but hadn't eaten anything since. Not surprising he was starving.

"Oh, you wouldn't be imposing," she said. "I'd be cooking for myself, anyway, so it's no trouble."

"You're very persuasive." He'd have to watch out.

"I've been told I'm quite stubborn," she said, lifting her chin.

"I can tell." Actually, he kind of liked that about her. And, really, it would be rude to refuse her offer. He knew she was just trying to help, as his aunt had wanted.

Making a snap decision he hoped he wouldn't regret, he stepped back and gestured Molly in. "You've talked me into dinner, on one condition."

She looked expectantly at him, her green eyes questioning. "Which is?"

"I don't want you to be waiting on me. So I'll help you get dinner together, okay?"

She paused, shaking her head, her curls swaying with the motion. "Oh, no, that's not necessary."

"I insist. You've had a long day, too, and I'm sure you're tired. If we work together, we can turn out a meal in no time." And he could get back to work faster, refueled and ready to tackle his code with fresh focus. Actually, if he ate a hearty meal, he'd probably get more work done. Another reason to agree to her deal.

"O...okay," she said, sounding strangely reluctant to agree. "I still have to drop the lures by Floyd's house, so I guess it would be nice to finish up here early."

"Exactly," Grant replied, nodding.

"Great. So, let's get started." She moved around him and headed toward the homey kitchen, her soft, breezy scent hitting him when she walked by.

Boy, she smelled good. Kind of like flowers in

a meadow, all sweet and warm and fresh. Suddenly, hanging out in the kitchen with her did sound great.

Uneasiness snaked through him. Maybe *too* great for a man who didn't want to get caught up in any woman ever again.

Molly unloaded the food for dinner onto Rose's tile kitchen counters, her hands so clumsy she almost dropped the loaf of French bread she'd brought.

She very deliberately set the bread on the counter, taking a deep breath to calm herself. She needed to simmer down and focus on finding out more about Grant so she could figure out who to set him up with.

Simple.

The thing was, cooking *for* Grant was a lot different than cooking *with* Grant.

That thought was reinforced when Grant entered the room, Jade at his heels adoringly, and he brought his charming self right into Molly's space. Yes, indeed. Rose's kitchen was small, Grant was big, and somehow preparing a meal together held the promise of a closeness that rattled her to no end. She wasn't here to act on any attraction she might feel. She was here to learn more about him to find his perfect match.

She gripped the edge of the counter, watching

Jade plop herself down in the corner and lay her head on her paws, her black eyes watching everything.

"What do you want me to do?" Grant asked, looking around the kitchen. He moved closer, then reached over and picked up a fat onion she'd unloaded. "You want me to demolish this baby?"

Trying to keep her wits about her, Molly zeroed in on the knife block to her right. She grabbed a big blade suitable for chopping. "Here you go," she said, handing it to him, careful not to touch his hand. She spied the cutting board next to the sink and picked it up. "You'll need this, too."

He put the knife down and took the board from her. "Okay. I've got tools. I'm sure I can figure out how to slice and dice."

She peered at him. "Have you ever chopped an onion?"

He shook his head as he retrieved the knife and held it up in the air. "No, I sure haven't."

"Um…you want me to show you how?" Chopping lessons seemed harmless enough.

He grabbed the onion and eyed it. "Nah, how hard can it be?"

Relief and disappointment hit her at once, creating a strange kind of off-balance feeling inside of her she didn't really like. She gestured to the cutting board. "Have at it, then. I only need half."

He threw the onion in the air and deftly caught

it with one hand, grinning. "Half a chopped onion for Chef Molly, coming right up."

My, he was cute. Put him in front of a grill with tongs in his hand and she was his.

Disconcerted all over again, Molly spun around and opened the refrigerator to hunt for salad makings.

Bent over, she rustled around in the fridge, then jerked one of the lower drawers out, pawing her way through the produce Rose had obviously bought for Grant.

"So," she said, focusing on her goal of learning as much as possible about Grant. "Do you read much?" She shoved a bag of baby carrots aside, searching for lettuce.

"Do I do what much?" Grant replied after a long moment.

"Read."

"Deed?"

"No, *read,* as in books," she yelled. Suddenly, a mental picture of herself developed in her brain, and the picture showed her hunched over, yelling into the refrigerator.

"Deed the rooks?"

Oh, brother. She grabbed the elusive lettuce at the bottom of the bin and straightened, chastising herself for being flustered. Grant was just a man, no more, no less. The fact that he was drop-dead gorgeous shouldn't matter.

She whirled around, shoving her hair out of her face. Time to be reliable and fulfill her promise to Rose by doing her matchmaker thing. Without acting like a twelve-year-old hanging out with her first crush.

She looked at Grant. He had his eyebrows drawn together and the knife suspended in midair. Obviously, he was puzzled by her behavior. Who could blame him?

He probably thought she was a bona fide nut job.

She smiled awkwardly, trying to look as if she hadn't just attempted to have a conversation with him while shouting into a kitchen appliance. "No. Read books."

"Oh," he said, nodding slowly. He went back to chopping, although he wielded the blade more like a machete than a knife. "Not really. I don't have time."

Right. Because he was always working. "Really? I'm a big reader." Although, since she wasn't looking for a match for herself, that discrepancy in their reading habits didn't matter. "Did you read as a kid?" she asked, heading across the kitchen to get a salad bowl from the cupboard.

"Yeah, I guess." More machete-ing. "Mostly science books."

That made sense. He was a brain, even though he didn't look like one.

"Oh, and comic books," he added. "I loved superheroes."

"Really? I read a lot of comic books as a kid, too. Who's your favorite?"

He stopped chopping and stared at her. "Spider Man, of course."

"Me, too," she replied, amazed that they had the same favorite. "No contest. My dogs' names are Peter and Parker, and I own the movie. How about you?"

"I only had time to see it once, but I loved it."

Of course. No time for movies in this guy's life. "You still have your comic books?"

He stilled, then quickly looked down. "My mom saved them, so they're up in my parents' attic somewhere."

Sympathy shot through her. Oh, yes. Rose had told her he'd recently lost his mom. "Have you ever thought about finding them?" she asked softly. "It might be fun to reread them sometime."

"Nope."

"Why not?" Wasn't it important for her to know lots about him? You know, to properly set him up.

Picking up the knife, he began to studiously chop the onion again, pausing before he quietly answered, "A lot of my mom's stuff is up there."

A knot built in her chest, making it hard to breathe. "Your aunt Rose told me about your mom. I'm so sorry."

"Thanks," he said, not looking up, his voice raw and husky. "It's been rough."

Her eyes burned. "My mom died when I was a little girl, so I know how hard it is to lose a mom." She'd been inconsolable for months after her mom had been killed in a car accident.

Grant looked up, his eyes full of empathy. "Oh, wow. How old were you?"

"Eight."

He shook his head. "That must have been really, really hard."

"It was." Harder still had been essentially losing her father, who had been so filled with grief over his wife's death, he'd forgotten all about Molly.

Until now. He'd been calling a lot recently, wanting back into her life. But the walls she'd put up wouldn't be so easily torn down. Even with God's help, and lots of prayers, she'd struggled with this issue for quite a while.

Suddenly, onion smell overwhelmed her, and her eyes started tearing. Drawing back, she actually looked at the pile of onions on the cutting board in front of Grant.

She did a double take. Instead of pieces of onion, the cutting board was full of onion mush, speckled with brown bits.

Her jaw went slack. "You didn't peel the onion before you chopped?" she asked, her throat burning.

He looked up, tears running down his sculpted cheeks. "No. Was I supposed to?" he asked, sniffing.

She backed away from the stinging onion aroma and nodded toward the mashed onions. "Uh... yeah. I thought you knew to take the dry, papery outer layer off."

He set the knife down and swiped at his eyes with the back of his hand before turning his watery gaze to his handiwork. "How would I know? I told you I've never chopped onions before."

"Good point." She gazed at the pile of goo that used to be an onion. "Um...you may have over-chopped a bit, too."

He considered the slush pile on the cutting board, his brow line hoisted high. "You think?"

She put her hands on her hips. "Definitely. They're supposed to be pieces, not...mush with skin."

He reached for the other half of the onion, his mouth curved into a wry smile. "You want me to try again? I'm game if you are, although we might end up onion-less." His eyes lit up. "Better yet, I'll do an internet search on how to chop onions."

She shook her head. "No, no need to bring your

computer into this. I'll do the chopping. Spaghetti sauce just wouldn't be right without onions." She glanced around and saw the antique table in the dining room off the kitchen. "Why don't you work on setting the table."

He set the onion down. "Now, *that* I can do." He picked up the knife and presented it to her with a flourish. "Your knife, Miss. Use it well."

She played along and accepted his "gift" with an exaggerated curtsy. "Thank you, kind sir."

Turning her attention to the onion, she chopped it on the cutting board next to the sink. She surreptitiously watched Grant rattle around the kitchen, gathering up the utensils and plates they'd need.

She couldn't help but notice how he moved with an easy male grace she found fascinating. Yes, he'd told her he spent a lot of time at his computer. But it was clear he spent some time working out, too. He was in terrific shape...um, for a computer nerd.

Suddenly, the knife bit into her finger with a sharp sting. "Ow!" She dropped the blade and jerked her hand away, looking down at the bleeding gash on her finger.

Dizziness engulfed her; the sight of blood had always made her woozy.

Grant was at her side in a flash. "What's wrong?"

At least she'd had the presence of mind to thrust

her hand out over the sink and underneath cold water rather than bleed all over Rose's kitchen. "I...cut my finger." *Because I was staring at you.*

"Let me see," he said, gently taking her hand.

She leaned his way for support, but squeezed her eyes shut, her teeth gritted. "I can't look."

"You've cut yourself pretty good," he said after a few moments, his voice laced with concern. A pause. "Keep your hand over the sink, okay? It's bleeding a lot."

She did as she was told, biting her lip against the fiery pain. Something dry engulfed her throbbing finger.

"I'm stopping the bleeding with a clean towel," he said.

"Okay," she said shakily. The ground tilted and her legs sagged.

He put one arm around her and guided her to the nearest kitchen chair. "Don't worry. I've got you."

She nodded as she sat. "Thanks. The sight of blood always gets to me."

He hunkered down next to her, still holding her towel-wrapped hand. "How's that?"

"Better," she replied, relaxing back in the chair. "My dizziness is passing."

"Good." Looking at her swaddled hand as he rose, he said, "Let's leave that on while I find the first-aid kit."

"Okay," she replied, taking a hold of the towel. "Check the linen closet in the hall. Rose keeps a lot of toiletries and stuff like that there."

"Will do," he said, leaving the kitchen.

While he was gone, Molly clenched her teeth at the pain in her index finger. Would she need stitches? She hoped not.

But she would need to quit staring at Grant.

A few moments later he returned, a bright orange first-aid bag in his hands. "Found it."

The concern in his eyes gave her tummy a little flip.

He sat down in the chair opposite her and reached out to take her injured hand. "Let's see what we have." Gingerly, he unwrapped the blood-stained towel from her hand.

Molly kept her gaze averted, flinching at the pain zinging through her finger.

She felt him lean in. "It looks pretty superficial," he said. "I'll just put some antibiotic ointment on it, bandage you up, and you'll be as good as new."

"Okay. Thanks." She peeked at her finger and her stomach heaved. She quickly turned away. "You sure it isn't worse? It feels like I gouged it pretty good."

He moved his chair, and himself, closer, then bent over her finger again, his gaze locked on her injury. "I'm positive. I know it hurts, but it isn't too bad."

"Whatever you say, Doctor Roderick," she said in a teasing tone, trying to distract herself from the pain.

He chuckled, glancing at her, his mouth curved up at the corners. "I'm no doctor, but I did have first-aid training in college. Will that do?"

"That'll work," she replied, doing her best to ignore his attractive smile.

"Good." He grabbed the ointment and gently dabbed it on her cut. Then he picked up a roll of gauze, unwound a length of the bandage material and cut it with the scissors he'd found in the kit.

As he worked to take care of her, Molly looked down at his bent head, noting his long eyelashes and sculpted cheekbones. Yes, he was one handsome guy. And caring and gentle, too.

Pulling her interested gaze away, she let him finish tending to her cut, doggedly refocusing her attention on her goal at hand—to figure him out so she could match him up with one of the many single and wonderful women in town. Maybe Phoebe…

After her finger was bandaged up tight, Molly was grateful Grant helped her finish making dinner. Clearly, he didn't have that much experience in the kitchen, but he took direction well and did a good job for a rookie.

Soon they were seated at Rose's antique dining room table, heaping plates of spaghetti before them.

"This looks—and smells—fantastic," Grant said, inhaling deeply. "I haven't had a home-cooked meal in a long time." Not surprising, given how hard he was working. One more reason she needed to find him his perfect match.

"Well, then, you were smart to let me stay." Molly took a piece of garlic bread from the cloth-covered bread basket with her good hand, then passed Grant the salad. "Eat up, there's plenty. And we made enough so you'll have leftovers for lunch tomorrow."

They ate in silence for a few minutes—she had to admit, she made a mean spaghetti sauce—and then the lack of conversation got to her, thanks to one too many silent, awkward meals with her dad.

Setting her fork on the edge of her plate, she regarded Grant. "So. What kind of project are you doing?"

He took a drink of water and put his glass down. "I'm writing computer code for a new client."

"So this…code job, it's very important?"

"Yes, very important. If I pull this project off in the ridiculously short amount of time I've been given, my company will secure the account for the future, and I'll get a huge promotion and a lot of respect within the software community."

Interesting. "Don't you get lonely working in such isolation?"

"Actually, no," Grant said, taking another piece of garlic bread from the basket. "I work on my time, when I want, with no distractions, no meaningless socializing."

She scrunched up her nose. Did Grant at least allow the Lord into his tiny box of a life? She'd be lost without His guidance.

"Being with people is not meaningless," Molly said emphatically. "I adore interacting with my customers, love helping them pick out products, forming attachments, making friends from all over the world. I've had customers from as far away as Hong Kong who still email me to chat." Granted, that was just email. But still, she was connected. Involved.

He blinked several times, as if her statement was so foreign to him he couldn't possibly understand where she was coming from. "Personally, I find a social life and business don't mix," he replied after a long moment.

He was making the same foolish choice as her father, the big-time corporate attorney.

"Sounds lonely," Molly said, shaking her head. Lonely and isolated. And faithless.

"Maybe so," Grant replied, pulling Molly back

into the conversation. "But some people like my kind of lifestyle."

Probably not his family. "Your bosses, for instance."

He laughed. "Definitely at the top of the list. But focusing on my job works for me because my career is my number-one priority. I don't have time for a social life, which is fine by me."

None of this made any sense to Molly. How could he live that way, always solitary, his only companion a computer? "So, your aunt Rose told me you don't have a girlfriend."

"Nope."

"I guess you don't have time, right?"

His expression closed. "Right. I gave up dating a long time ago."

She almost blurted, "Me, too," but she held back the words just in time. She was trying to find the perfect woman for him, not reaffirm his reasons to stay isolated with her own sob stories.

With her promise to Rose in mind, she said, "I was wondering if you'd like to go to church with me on Christmas Eve, the week after next? I'm sure you'd love the service."

Grant froze, his fork midway to his mouth. Then he very deliberately set the utensil down. "Church isn't really my thing," he said evenly. Too evenly. As if he was trying to suppress something painful and had gone all blank instead.

She blinked. "Oh. Okay. No big deal." Not a believer, then? Again, another clue to his personality. She was slowly finding out about the real man beneath the attractive exterior. Good. Yet...not.

Not surprisingly, Grant changed the subject. "So, how long have you lived in Moonlight Cove?"

"Three years. I moved here when I graduated from the University of Oregon."

"How did you end up in this neck of the woods?"

"My family and I used to vacation here when I was little." In fact, Moonlight Cove was the last place her family had spent any happy time before her mother died.

"Lots of good memories, I bet," he said.

Actually, her only good memories of her childhood centered around Moonlight Cove. "Tons," she said, bending the truth. A lot. She was ashamed to admit how limited her happy childhood memories actually were. As in almost nonexistent.

"I have good memories here, too," he said. "I came here every summer to visit Aunt Rose when I was growing up."

"That must have been fun."

Again, his expression shuttered. "It was."

He seemed uncomfortable with the conversation, so she decided not to push him on the subject and instead focused on eating. Grant seemed content to simply chow down.

A few minutes later, he set his utensils neatly on his plate and said, "Dinner was fantastic. I could get used to this kind of delicious cooking in a hurry."

A warm glow of pride settled in Molly's chest. It was always nice to please someone who could express himself with words, not barks. "Thanks." And then she thought, *Note to self: fix him up with someone who likes to cook.*

They rose and began to clean up, and when Grant went to take the garbage out, she ran through all the information about him she'd collected today. He liked superheroes. He was reluctant to date. He appreciated home cooking. And he was a runner.

Who should she set him up with?

Of course, she'd already set her matchmaking sights on Phoebe; she might be the perfect match. If that didn't fly, there was also Anna Stevens, who owned Moonlight Cove Bakery on Main Street. She was single, and was the best baker in town, hands down.

Then a rogue thought crashed through Molly's mind.

On paper, another person also had a lot in common with him.

And that person was…her.

She looked heavenward.

Hello? God? Looks like I have another problem I'm going to need Your help with.

Chapter Three

The next day, Grant glowered at the naughty dog sitting in front of his desk. "You're driving me crazy."

Jade had spent the morning alternating between barking at the squirrels in the backyard from the window, dropping her gross tennis ball in his lap and asking to go out every ten minutes, which not only distracted him, but required that he wipe her muddy paws off every time she came in.

She lifted her furry face. There it was, that dog smile she kept giving him. It was as if she could actually understand him.

He snorted and rolled his eyes. *Yeah, right, Roderick.* Maybe his killer work schedule had fried his brain. She was just a dog, albeit a very, very smart one.

He had to get some peace and quiet, or he'd never make his deadline.

Before he could figure out how to accomplish the seemingly impossible goal, his cell phone rang.

Grant pulled the phone out of his pocket and looked at the display. Dad. He and his dad were close, and Grant always looked forward to their three-times-a-week conversations.

Grant pushed the answer button. "Hey, Dad," he said. "How are you?"

A pause. "I'm fine. And you?"

Grant's stomach clenched. Dad wasn't fine at all, and hadn't been since Grant's mother had died after a long, agonizing battle with breast cancer a year ago. Neither he nor his dad had really come to terms with losing Naomi Roderick.

"Are you sure you're fine?" Grant asked, wishing he lived closer to his dad in Portland. He might have cut romantic relationships from his life in favor of work, but he was still really close to Dad.

"Ah, well, I'm just…a little lonely, that's all."

The softly spoken words shredded Grant's heart. His dad wasn't recovering well from his wife's death, and Grant wondered if he ever would. The once vibrant man had shriveled inside, and it seemed only a shell was left.

"You said you were going to look into volunteering somewhere," Grant said, trying to sound as upbeat as he could. "How's that going?"

"Oh, nothing really appeals to me," his dad said, his voice subdued. Hollow. "I'd rather stay home."

Grant sighed. "Have you gone to church lately?" At one time, his dad had found solace in the church.

"Nah, not yet." A long silence. "It just wouldn't be the same without your mother."

Grant's eyes burned. His dad was right. How could Grant ask him to look to God for comfort when Grant himself couldn't do it? "I know, Dad." Nothing had been the same since his mom had died. She'd been the heart of the Roderick family.

A wave of fresh grief washed over Grant. He slammed it down.

"Maybe I'll go next week," his dad mumbled.

"That sounds like a plan."

Grant decided to drop the subject and avoid the pain for both himself and his dad for now. Anything more was beyond him. "Listen, as soon as I'm done with this project, I'll come down for the weekend. Maybe we can go fishing."

"Okay, that'd be great," his dad said, but Grant could tell his heart wasn't in his words.

They talked about a few other mundane subjects, then said goodbye and hung up. Grant sat for a few moments, concern for his dad oozing through him. They shared their grief, but Grant didn't know how to deal with his own, much less his dad's. He was at a total loss as to how to help. And with Christmas coming up, things would only get worse.

His mom had *loved* Christmas. Which was why he hadn't accepted Molly's invitation to go to church. He just couldn't face a Christmas Eve service without his mom.

Jade barked at the window—the squirrels in the yard driving her bonkers again—jerking Grant's thoughts back to the problem at hand. Aside from putting a muzzle on the dog, how was he going to get the uninterrupted quiet he needed?

He glanced outside, noting that it was cloudy and windy, but not raining. Maybe Jade needed a long walk to take the edge off her canine crazies. They could stop by Molly's store and buy a new toy or two to distract Jade for the rest of the day. Sounded like a plan.

He hoped for Jade's sake his strategy worked.

If it didn't, it might mean a reservation at the local kennel. For the dog, of course.

Saying a fervent prayer under her breath, Molly let out a long-suffering sigh, her hands stiff on the computer keyboard. Why in the world hadn't she taken more computer classes in college?

She'd spent the last two hours holed up in the back room of the store, trying to retrieve some tax files from her hard drive for the IRS audit scheduled for the day after tomorrow.

Two tear-her-hair-out hours with nothing to show but a fizzled brain, a throbbing headache and a sudden, burning desire to heave her computer through the window. Not to mention typing was tricky—and slow—with a bandaged finger.

She looked through the list of virtual folders again, including the one named TAX FILES. Nothing. The files were gone.

She shot to her feet and began to pace, rubbing her temple. What in the world was she going to do? The audit was in less than two days' time. She was a total computer idiot. She'd looked in every nook and cranny of her computer to no avail. And, unfortunately, she hadn't backed up her data.

This problem could spell disaster for her business.

Worse, a town the size of Moonlight Cove wasn't exactly a hotbed of computer repair options. Far from it. There was one guy who was good, and it was common knowledge he was scheduled weeks out. No help there.

She chewed on her lip. Maybe she could ask Computer Man Grant to help…no, no, he was busy with his own work and wouldn't be able to spare the time. Drat.

Just when she was about to spontaneously combust from anxiety she heard the buzzer on the front door go off, signaling the arrival of a customer. Glad for the distraction, she headed out front to relieve Gena. She closed the door to the back room, leaving Peter and Parker napping there.

Molly's eyebrows shot up—and so did her heart rate—when she saw the unexpected pair who'd just walked in.

She turned to Gena. "I'll handle this one. Why don't you go take a break."

Gena shrugged, grabbed her purse and went out the front door, her brunette ponytail swinging.

Molly headed to where Grant stood by the front counter. He was trying, in vain, to contain a wild Jade, who was acting pretty rambunctious, jumping up and down, woofing.

"Jade, sit!" Molly commanded, her dog training instincts kicking in.

Jade sat.

Molly grabbed a treat from her jeans pocket. "Good girl," she said, giving Jade the treat. She cocked an eyebrow, then looked at Grant. "Is it my imagination, or is she particularly wild today?"

Grant rubbed his jaw, shaking his head. "Wild isn't even the word. It hasn't been a good morning."

"I'm with you there," Molly replied. "It's been a rough morning here, as well." Normally she was a good business problem solver, but today…well, not so much. She was a people person, not a computer whiz.

Grant studied her, his eyes alight with concern. "What's wrong?" His gaze dropped to her bandaged finger. "Is your cut bothering you?"

His worry about her injury touched her. "Oh, no. Nothing like that."

"Oh, good." He drew his eyebrows together. "Then what's up?"

"The thing is…I'm having a major computer problem," she said sheepishly.

His ears perked up at the word *computer.* "What's wrong?"

"Well, I'm being audited the day after tomorrow, and I can't find the files I need for the IRS agent on my computer." As she talked, she bent down and unhooked Jade from her leash. "They're just…gone."

He instantly went into techie mode. "Where are your backup files?"

"Um…I didn't exactly back up my stuff."

Classic rookie mistake. "Why not?"

"I forgot?"

Sighing, he said, "Bet you'll back up from now on, won't you?"

She made an *X* with her fingers over her heart. "I promise."

He looked at his watch. Where had the day gone? "You want me to take a look?" He didn't really have time, but the thought of leaving her floundering with the IRS breathing down her neck didn't sit well with him.

"Oh, no, I know you're on a tight schedule."

"I can spare some time," he said. Not exactly true, but close enough.

"Are you sure?" she asked, her green eyes starting to glow with hope. "I hate to impose...."

"I'm sure," he said. "I can probably track down the files in a half hour or so."

"You think?" She touched his arm. "Oh, that would be great. And I tell you what. Since you're doing me a favor, why don't I take Jade off your hands for the next few days? She can hang out here with me, Peter and Parker during the day."

Relief shot through him, taking his mind off the warm spot on his arm where she'd touched him. Dog problem solved. "That'd be great." Definitely worth an hour, tops, of his time.

"You have time to take a look now?" she asked.

He gestured to the back room where he'd seen her desktop computer yesterday. "Lead the way."

Just as he started to follow her back there, the door buzzer went off again. He and Molly turned in unison, and Jade let out a happy *woof* and ran to greet their visitor.

Phoebe walked into the store. She bent down and gave Jade a good ear scratching, then straightened and headed their way, waving colored papers in her hand.

"Hey, Phoebs," Molly called. "I bet you've got flyers, don't you?"

"I sure do, all made up for our Christmas specials," she said, handing him and Molly each a bright red piece of paper. An impish grin took over Phoebe's mouth. "In honor of the holiday, our flavor of the month is Candy Cane, and it's really good. Buy one scoop, get one free through the end of the year." Phoebe gave Molly a wide-eyed, unblinking look. "Maybe you two could stop in together sometime soon."

Molly pursed her lips and glared at Phoebe. "Or maybe Grant could stop by and you two could have ice cream together."

"I'd be working," Phoebe said matter-of-factly. "No time for socializing."

"Oh, and I have unlimited amounts of time for hanging out and eating ice cream?" Molly retorted, flipping her hair, her green eyes flashing like emeralds.

Grant hesitated, puckering his forehead, his gaze swinging back and forth between Phoebe and Molly. What was going on?

Then they both spoke at once, their words mixing up until he couldn't understand either of them.

"Whoa, whoa, ladies," he said after a few seconds of verbal mayhem, holding up both hands.

They both abruptly stopped talking and swung their gazes toward him.

"What's up?" He put his hands on his hips. "I feel as if there's some weird subtext playing out here that, frankly, I don't really understand."

Neither woman spoke. Instead, they just kind of glared at each other, their mouths tight.

Finally, Phoebe huffed, flopped the flyers down on the counter with a *whap* and said, "I guess I'll warn you, since Molly will strike before you know what's coming."

"Warn me? Strike?" He grimaced. "What in the world are you talking about, since I doubt we're on the subject of war games here?"

"Molly's our resident matchmaker, and she's quite good at it." As she spoke, Phoebe unbuttoned her coat. "If you're not careful, she'll have you and me talking china patterns by the end of the week."

Cold-edged surprise bounced like a rock through Grant. He turned to Molly, his jaw tight, his brow line raised so high he doubted he had eyebrows. "Is this true?"

She wouldn't meet his gaze and remained suspiciously silent. Just tongue-tied? Or guilty as charged?

He was confident it was the latter.

* * *

Despite the store being kept at a very temperate seventy degrees, burning warmth flared in Molly's cheeks as she tried to look anywhere but at Grant's accusing stare.

Uneasiness poked her. Maybe her matchmaker idea hadn't been a good one, after all. Or maybe she should have told him about her plan, even though that wasn't usually the way she worked.

"Yes. Yes, it is true," Molly answered honestly. Lying had never been her style. "I'm a matchmaker on the side."

He looked at Phoebe, seemingly for confirmation.

"She thinks I should be dating," Phoebe said matter-of-factly, a brow quirked.

His gaze came back to Molly, then narrowed. "When were you going to clue me in?" he asked, his voice edged in steel.

She squirmed. Oh, boy. Why did she feel so… guilty? She'd had only good intentions. But maybe a man who didn't date wouldn't see things her way. Hindsight was always twenty-twenty.

"Soon," she said in a placating tone. She continued on, feeling the need to explain why she hadn't told him about her plan. "But I've found I can make better matches if the people I'm matching don't know exactly what I'm doing right away."

Grant frowned, then looked at the floor, shaking his head.

Molly's bravado faltered. She liked his smile and direct gaze better than his obvious disconcertion. A lot better.

Phoebe stepped forward and piped in. "Actually, that's true. She gets what she calls 'love hunches' and usually finds ways to get people together pretty much out of nowhere."

"Love hunches?" Grant's brow knitted. "Care to explain?"

At least he was interested in her romantic intuition, rather than simply scoffing and writing her talent off as ridiculous right off the bat. "Certainly. Since I moved here, I've discovered that I have the ability to…know who would be a good love match for whom."

He crossed his arms over his broad chest. "How do you know this?"

"It's hard to explain…."

"Try," he said levelly.

His serious tone took her aback. She nodded, wanting to salvage what she could of her pride. "My love hunches are just a…feeling I get every so often."

He paused, seemingly to mull over what she'd said. Finally, he said, "Someone besides me can't possibly know what I'm feeling at any given time." He looked away, then swung his gaze back to Molly. "Don't you tell people when you're working away behind their backs, figuring all of this out?"

Molly swallowed. "See, the thing is, I can get a better idea of a person's personality if they're—"

"Clueless?" Grant said, cocking that brow again.

"Well…yes." Sounded worse than it was. "Once someone knows I'm trying to figure them out, they clam up and act funny. The other person will only see what I see if both act naturally. Like their true selves."

He paused again, obviously digesting what she'd said.

Molly glanced at Phoebe, grimacing speculatively as if to ask whether he was going to twirl his finger next to his temple to show how loony he thought she was.

With a lift of her slim shoulders, Phoebe grimaced back as if to say she had no earthly idea what he was going to do.

Molly held her breath, hoping he wouldn't dismiss her as a kook.

She didn't want him to think badly of her; she needed his help with her computer problem. Yes. Exactly. Alienating him now would be a mistake.

Finally, he spoke. "Was my aunt in on this?"

"Kind of," Molly replied. "She asked me to be sure you got out some while you were here. To me, that means fixing you up." True enough. "And really, most young, unattached guys would jump at the chance to meet nice, eligible women."

"I'm not most guys," Grant said.

No kidding.

"And I told you I'm not interested in dating, right?" he added.

She nodded slowly. "Yes, but not until last night." Splitting hairs, but it was all she had to justify her actions.

"Okay, I'll give you that one," he said, tilting his head to the side. "But you were still planning on fixing me up with Phoebe, here, weren't you?"

"Yes."

"Well, I'm going to have to ask you to cross that idea off your list. I don't want to be fixed up on any dates, with anybody, all right?"

Fear of her attraction to him had her saying, "Are you sure? It can't be good to hole up all by yourself for days on end." Regretting the implications of her statement, she quickly added, "And Phoebe's really quite nice."

Phoebe made a noise she covered quickly with a cough, but she couldn't hide the laughter in her eyes.

Grant quirked a grin at Phoebe. "I'm sure you are," he said to her before he turned his attention back to Molly. "But the fact remains, I don't date."

Molly opened her mouth to speak. "Yes, but—"

He cut her off. "And even if I did date, I don't have time while I'm in town. I have a killer deadline, remember? I need to be working. Not dating."

"I remember." How could she forget? She'd heard the same excuse from her father so many times while she'd been growing up, she'd lost count.

Remembered pain filtered through her at the thought of how many times her dad had left to "take care of things at work" instead of staying home with her.

"So you'll back off on the matchmaking stuff?" Grant asked. "I'm here to help you with your computer, not find a date."

After a moment, she simply nodded. She couldn't force him to date, any more than she could force herself.

"Well, then, I suppose I can find a way to forgive you for not being completely honest with me."

Immense relief spread through her. But not because he wouldn't be dating anyone else. No, no, no. Because she needed his help with a problem. Nothing more than that.

He pointed to the back room. "Let's get back on track and take a look at your computer. Tick-tock."

"Okay." Excellent idea. Oddly, all this talk of Grant dating had her feeling...weirdly off balance.

She turned to Phoebe. "Can we reschedule our lunch for tomorrow?"

"Of course," Phoebe said with a wide smile that Molly found strange. "I'll call you later."

Frowning slightly at Phoebe's grin, Molly said, "Great." She gestured to Grant to precede her to the back room. "Let's get started."

He walked by and Molly started to follow.

Phoebe caught her arm. "Moll."

Molly stopped, gazing inquisitively at her friend.

"You are so cooked, girl."

"What do you mean?"

"Why did you agree so easily to stop trying to fix Grant up?"

"Um...because he asked me to?"

Phoebe scoffed. "Yeah, right." Clearly, she wasn't buying Molly's answer.

"You heard him," Molly replied. "He asked me to stop, so I will."

Phoebe grabbed her hat and put it on. "Do you remember how many times Warren Stone asked you to quit setting him up with Janice?"

"Yes. Of course I do. Six times, to be exact."

"And did you stop?"

"No. And thank goodness I didn't. They're happily married now, and Warren has thanked me profusely many times since they found each other."

"True. But my point is, you don't usually listen to people when they ask you to stop matchmaking."

Vague uneasiness flitted through Molly. "So?"

"So, I think you have another reason for taking off your matchmaker's hat without much of a fight."

Molly tightened her jaw. Miss Perceptive—aka Phoebe—wasn't going to let this go. Molly needed to face Phoebe's pontifications head-on or Phoebe would never let the matter die.

"Did it ever occur to you that I backed off because I need his help with my computer?" Molly asked in a whisper, nodding toward the back room.

"Yes, it did," Phoebe replied evenly. "But I also think you backed off because deep down you don't want Grant to date anyone else."

"And why would I care about that?" Molly asked, her voice just a teensy bit too high for a woman who needed to present an indifferent front—both to herself and to Phoebe.

Phoebe leaned in and whispered, "Because you want to date the man yourself."

Grant sat down at Molly's small wooden desk and booted up her older but serviceable desktop computer.

As he waited for her, he saw Phoebe lean in and whisper something to Molly. Molly waved a hand in the air, shaking her head vigorously, and then Phoebe laughed, said something else and headed out of the store.

Molly stood for a second, obviously spoke to herself, and then he saw her take a visible deep breath, almost as if she were calming down.

He needed to do the same, but he resisted the urge to talk to himself in favor of simply mulling over what Molly had tried to do.

Her matchmaking efforts had really taken him off guard. He had no intention of reviving his romantic life anytime soon. If ever. And, really, as long as he could deflect her efforts to set him up, why should it matter what Molly threw at him?

Swiping a hand over his face, he forced himself not to delve too deeply into that question. He just needed to figure out what was wrong with her computer, fix it and get back to work at Aunt Rose's. Fast.

Good plan.

Molly arrived, Jade at her heels, and Molly's smooth cheeks looked a tad pink.

"Everything okay?" he asked as he rolled the chair back toward the door so she could get to the computer. She had to go around Peter, Parker and Jade, who were now piled onto the large dog bed in the corner.

She pulled in her chin. "Everything's fine. Why?"

"You were talking to yourself back there."

"Oh. I do that." She gave him a goofy grin. "Weird, huh?"

Before he could stop himself, he asked, "What were you and Phoebe talking about?"

Molly waved a hand in the air. "Oh, Phoebe has the funny idea that *I* should be dating you."

Surprise bounced through him. "Really?"

Molly clicked on something on the computer screen, then straightened and turned. She opened the mini-fridge next to her desk, grabbed a water and offered it to him.

He took it. "Thanks."

She got a water for herself, then twisted the lid open and took a swig. After she swallowed, she said, "Yes, really. Phoebe's a hopeless romantic at heart, but she knows I don't date."

"Why not?" He imagined someone as attractive and nice as Molly would have more dates than she knew what to do with, even in tiny Moonlight Cove.

"I've been dumped a lot," she said bluntly.

That surprised him. Who would dump her? "No way."

"Way." Her jawline tightened. "Nothing hurts more than having someone you love leave you," she said, her eyes intent on the computer screen.

He knew that story, could have written it, actually. "I totally agree," he said, nodding emphatically. "I've been there, and being the dumpee isn't fun."

Molly pointed at him. "Exactly. So that's why I'm not interested in dating you, or anyone, for that matter. I've decided love isn't worth the risk or pain. I'm much happier on my own."

"Ditto." He'd graduated from the School of Heartbreak, and he was never walking those dangerous halls again.

She put a hand on his shoulder and squeezed. "I'm so glad you understand."

He did his best to ignore the warm, tingly spot where she'd touched him on his shoulder. He cleared his throat. Twice. Then he forced his mind back to why he was here. "So, about your computer..."

The front door buzzer went off, signaling the arrival of a customer. The dogs jumped up and ran out front.

"Sorry, I have to get that. I'll be right back." Molly turned and headed out of the office, her red curls bouncing, her scent washing over him like a fresh spring breeze as she walked by.

He watched her go, admitting to himself that she was very attractive, and sweet, too. In another life, he'd probably be all over dating her.

He laughed humorlessly under his breath. *Get a grip, bud.*

No way was he going to risk his work goals for a woman. Molly was a distraction he didn't need, now or ever. And she wasn't interested in him, period. He had to remember that while he was in town.

No matter how appealing she proved to be.

Chapter Four

"Let me know how Sweet Pea likes that food," Molly said to Ray Burton, a longtime customer. "If she won't eat that kibble, just return the bag and we'll try something else."

"Will do, Molly." Ray flipped the hood of his rain jacket up onto his head over his close-cropped gray hair. "She's picky as all get-out, so we'll see."

Ray stepped through the door into the gray winter drizzle that had started early in the day and hadn't let up. Molly waved goodbye as the glass door closed, then snuck a surreptitious glance toward the back room where her handsome computer technician waited.

Her tummy did a little flip; mighty small quarters back there with Grant. And all that talk of dating and compatibility—and Phoebe's comment about Molly wanting to date Grant—had really thrown Molly. Phoebe was very perceptive and usually hit the mark with her observations.

But not this time. Molly wasn't interested in Grant; she was all about protecting her heart. Fortunately, Phoebe had backed off.

For now, but probably not forever, Molly realized with dismay. Phoebe was stubborn and didn't tend to let things go. But she'd met her match, Molly vowed. She could be mule-headed, too, when necessary. She'd have to prove she wasn't interested in Grant with her actions.

No problem.

She hastily dropped the stuffed fox dog toy she'd somehow picked up, then fiddled absently with some paperwork next to the cash register, pretending to be busy for a moment, quickly planning how to handle Grant being here, all over her space.

Okay. No biggie. She'd just show him the computer problem, wait in the main part of the store while he fixed things and then usher him out. And that would be that.

As for his charming ways and gorgeous blue eyes…well, she'd have to find a way to ignore those. Whatever it took.

Bracing herself, she headed to the back room, putting her "Grant" shields in place.

She noted that the dogs were back on the bed

in the corner and Grant was already working on her computer. Boy, he didn't waste any time.

He glanced up from the screen. "You really should password protect your computer. I just opened up your files, no problem."

"You really think that's necessary?"

"For sure I do." He gestured to the flat-screen computer monitor. "I'm guessing you have all of your work stuff on here?"

Picking up her water bottle, she nodded.

He pulled his face into a stern expression, which somehow only made him look cuter. "Well, without a password, someone could just boot this thing up, have a look around and access anything they wanted—financial records, addresses, tax files—you name it. Not to mention the danger of identity theft."

Okay. She deserved the dig about the missing tax stuff. She'd been lazy and hadn't backed up. He obviously knew what he was talking about, and she *did* need to protect her files.

"Okay, okay. I get the message. I'll add a password. And I'll start making duplicate files of everything." She started looking around. "I have a thumb drive around here somewhere."

"Be sure and give it to me before I leave." Pointing to the computer, he said, "Let's just do the password thing now." He clicked the mouse a few times, then turned and looked up at her expectantly. "What'll it be? And don't use *Peter* or *Parker*. Pet names are a bad choice."

She raised her chin. "Isn't a password supposed to be a secret?" He'd given her a hard time about her lack of computer security. Fine. She could be the most security-minded woman in town.

He looked mildly offended. "What? You don't trust me?"

Actually, she did trust him. With her computer. "I barely know you," she said instead.

"Well…I'm Rose's nephew."

"Still…" She shook her head. "To be truly secure, nobody but me should know the magic word, right?"

"Yes, but I'm going to need to know it to do my thing, so…"

She paused.

"How about we choose something now, and you can change it to something super-secret later," he said.

"Okay. But let me do it so I'll know how next time."

He stood up, stepped back and motioned toward her computer. "Good idea."

"Thank you." She scooched around Grant as best she could without touching him, which was tricky, given the close quarters. And the fact that as she moved close, she could tell he smelled really, really good.

Flustered by his proximity, and distracted by his spicy, dizzying scent, she sat hurriedly before she had herself completely turned around—and knocked the rolling chair with her right leg.

She tried to go with the program and sit anyway, but the chair was crooked, she was unbalanced…and she found nothing but air. She let out a yelp of surprise as she began to fall, flailing ungracefully.

Thankfully, Grant's strong arms reached out and caught her before she hit the floor.

"Whoa!" he exclaimed, hoisting her up with care, as if she weighed nothing at all. "I've got you." He set her upright on her feet, his hands securely around her waist, sending disturbing tingles up her spine.

Once she regained her footing, her first instinct was to jump away from his disconcerting touch. But with the computer table in front of her and Grant filling up every molecule of space behind her, there was absolutely nowhere to go.

"You okay?" he asked, leaning around, still touching her, steadying her with his tight but gentle grip.

Turning, she found him inches away, looking at her with a concerned gaze.

She fought staring into his stunning sapphire-tinted eyes and tried to settle her racing heart. "I…I'm fine," she said breathlessly as she attempted to stand on her own and get away from his devastating everything.

She succeeded, but her legs were shaky, as if she'd run a couple hundred miles.

"Here," he said, nudging the chair toward her with his knee. He moved his hands to her shoulders, then gently pushed down. "Why don't you sit."

She complied and sat with a *plop*, hoping the chair was actually underneath her this time. This was better. "Okay, I'm fine now."

But his big, warm hands stayed on her shoulders, heating her from the inside out, the sensation decidedly pleasant.

"You sure?" She felt him lean down again, moving into her space. "You seem a little shaky," he said close to her ear.

A little? Try a quivering mess. "Nah, I'm good," she replied, trying to sound as if his touch didn't affect her at all. As if she wasn't about to dissolve into a boneless puddle right there on her office floor.

His hands tightened again, gently pressing her shoulders.

Before he could reply, she blurted, "You can take your hands off now." She eased away from him as best she could without jamming her nose into her computer screen.

He complied with an unintelligible exclamation.

Setting her hands on the keyboard, she focused in on the task at hand and tried to think of a password. But her mind went blank; all she could think about was Grant standing behind her. Watching.

"The first-most-used password is 1 2 3 4 5 6," he said, "so don't choose that. And don't choose the word *password,* either. Believe it or not, it's the second-most-used password."

She stared at him for a long moment, her jaw slack, amazed. "Wow. You actually *know* this kind of stuff."

He shrugged. "Yup."

"You are a wealth of odd data, my friend."

"What can I say? I'm a blast at product launches."

"I'm sure," she replied, turning around to face the computer, smiling, then quickly frowning. Since when did she find knowledge of computer trivia so charming?

Determined to not let Grant's surprisingly appealing quirks distract her, she put her hands back in type position. But her mind remained irritatingly blank about a good password.

But thinking about a good *man*...well, that seemed to be easy with Grant around.

She shook her head, as if she could dislodge that thought from her mind. "Um...I'm coming up blank."

Leaning down, he put his hand on the desk,

close to hers. "I suggest a 'word' that is a mix of lower-and uppercase characters, numbers and punctuation marks."

"Great." Seeing as how she couldn't seem to come up with anything at the moment, his idea was a good one.

"So, what was the name of the street you grew up on?"

"Daisy Street."

"So how about *D A I $ Y $ T R & & T?*"

"Sounds perfect." She slowly entered the password, avoiding using her bandaged finger as best she could, then reentered it. All set.

"You think you can remember that?" he asked.

"I hope so." She frowned, then reached for a scratch pad and pen. "Maybe I should write it down."

He covered her hand with his big, warm one before she could write anything. His touch made her breathing snag. She turned her gaze up to him, widening her eyes.

He seemed to catch himself, then removed his hand. "Um…you should never write your password down." He tapped his head. "I have a memory for these kinds of things, though, so if you forget it, just ask and I'll be happy to remind you."

A warm glow settled in the vicinity of her chest to match the toasty feeling his hand left behind.

"Your know-how means a lot to me," she said truthfully. "I really appreciate you sticking around to help me out of this mess."

"It's no big deal."

"Yes, it is. I would be in big trouble without your expertise, and I know you have a tight deadline."

He regarded her speculatively, then crossed his arms over his broad chest. "Actually, I'm surprised you let me help."

"Why?" she asked warily.

"Well, I may be off base, but it seems to me that you're usually the one helping out, and that you don't ask for help yourself very often."

She blinked, surprised and a bit uneasy with his perceptiveness. She rarely asked for or expected assistance from others, having had to be self-sufficient since she was very young.

And explaining that would mean talking about her neglected childhood, which was something she didn't do often. Or ever, really. Admitting her dad had basically ignored her for most of her childhood was difficult. Even Phoebe didn't know the details of how neglectful Molly's dad had been.

After a long, thoughtful pause, she decided that it couldn't hurt to answer his question in very general terms, which would contribute to the conversation in a friendly way without revealing her private pain. Or making him uncomfortable. She was sure the last thing he'd want to hear about was her family drama.

"I've had to depend on only myself for a long time," she said, choosing her words very carefully. "So I'm used to handling things alone."

No understatement. Her dad had fulfilled his financial obligations toward her when he'd paid for college expenses, but that had been it for him. No driving lessons at sixteen. No warnings about boys with fast cars and faster hands, and certainly no emotional support.

"No family, then?" Grant asked. "You told me your mom died when you were a kid. Is your dad around?"

She averted her gaze, trying to hide the ache inside that his question caused. "He lives in Portland," she said. "But we're...not really close." As in they'd barely spoken about anything truly important in years.

Oh, sure, he called now and then to "talk"— more so lately—but their conversations remained superficial. Though she asked God for guidance on the matter often, she just couldn't find a way to forgive her dad for emotionally abandoning her back when her mom had died.

"Any reason you're not close?" Grant asked softly.

She felt her walls go up. Grant was unintentionally probing at a raw wound. Why, though? Maybe he was a fixer of people as well as computers. Seemed unlikely, given he was a bit of a loner. Was he just making small talk?

"Oh, I don't know," she said, trying to sound breezy rather than sad; no need to drag him into a deep discussion about her personal struggles. Or expose her ugly warts. "He has his life, I have mine. We just don't seem to have time to get together much."

"So you're okay with all of that?"

Not really. But she didn't know how to forgive her dad and wasn't sure she wanted to. And prayer hadn't helped.

"I'm used to it," she said, being truthful, yet deliberately vague. Their conversation was zooming into painful personal territory, and that wasn't a place she wanted to go. "I have lots of friends here in town, so I manage just fine."

"But you're usually the one helping all of those friends when they need someone to lean on, right?"

She mustered a smile, attempting to look carefree and light rather than admit to how alone she sometimes felt. "I just like to be there for people. But don't worry. I'm happy with my life the way it is."

Not exactly true all of the time, but close enough. Everyone had their problems, right? Look at Phoebe. She'd lost her fiancé, and she still managed to get through the day. Compared to Phoebe's trials, Molly truly believed she had it easy. Who was she to complain?

"Good," Grant said. "Somehow the thought of you all alone, with no one to help you when you need it, bothers me."

His caring about her well-being touched her; a small part of her wished she had a man like him, someone who would support her when things got rough. But that would mean letting him into her life and heart, and that, as she'd discovered in the past, would be a mistake. She was better off on her own. When she needed help, she'd look to the Lord.

"Well, thanks, I appreciate your concern." She gestured around with one hand. "But as you can see, I'm doing just fine, so you can rest easy that I'll be okay."

He stared at her, looking as if he were trying to figure out if she was leveling with him or not. Then he said, "Great."

Just as she was beginning to wonder if he was really worried about her, he said, "Let's get back to your computer problem." He looked at his watch, then frowned slightly. "Tick-tock. I need to wrap this up and get back to my work."

She breathed an internal sigh of relief. Now

maybe he'd let the subject go and she could relax. Sort of. "Sounds good," she said.

As they talked about the missing files, she realized his needing to get back to work reminded her that though Grant was obviously a considerate, caring guy, his priority would always be his job.

And that was too much like her dad for her ever to give in to her attraction to Grant. No matter how much she might daydream about that exact thing more often than she liked.

Chapter Five

Grant watched Molly head back out to the main part of the store to assist a customer. A knot of concern tightened in his chest.

What he'd said was true; he didn't like the thought of Molly not asking for the same help for herself that she so freely gave to others. Everybody needed support once in a while, and he couldn't think of a time in his life when his parents hadn't been there for him.

Truthfully, he'd sensed an underlying sadness when Molly had talked about her shaky relationship with her dad, even though she'd sounded outwardly fine with the disconnect between them.

Grant rubbed his face. He couldn't imagine being truly fine with that kind of situation. Family was precious; nothing had hit that home better for him than losing his mom.

But, realistically, what could he do about Molly

and her dad's estrangement? It was none of his business, really, and he was no relationship expert. In fact, besides being close to his immediate family, he was wary of most other personal relationships. He was the last person who should be giving Molly advice.

Besides, he wasn't looking to be involved with Molly in any kind of truly personal way; he could fix her computer, yes, but that had to be it.

Yeah, he needed to ignore his odd need to help her and focus on getting her computer problem solved as quickly as possible so he could get back to work. He had an important deadline looming; he didn't have time for much else. He had to remember that.

With that thought foremost in his mind, he turned his attention to finding her lost files. Fast.

He clicked quickly around her computer directory, attempting to diagnose the issue and figure out why she couldn't access the files she needed.

But he still couldn't stay focused on the data popping up on the screen in front of him. An hour and not much progress later, his gaze again returned to the main store area and the red-headed woman running the place like a gregarious dynamo of the Moonlight Cove doggy supply chain.

It didn't help that the dogs jumped up from their

shared bed and ran out to the main part of the store every time the door buzzer went off.

As his attention was drawn to her time and time again, he couldn't help but be impressed by her interpersonal skills and sales know-how. Clearly, she was good at what she did, as she was so helpful and friendly to the customers, offering heartfelt advice and guidance. All the while selling a ton of dog stuff to what seemed like every dog lover in town.

It was obvious she really loved her job. And based on the number of *non*–dog owners stopping by to ask Molly's advice, this town loved *her*.

She'd evidently worked hard to make her business a success. As a results-driven, ambitious person himself, he really liked and admired that about her.

And it didn't take a genius to see that she had a way with the dogs that came in with their owners. Every canine who scampered through the door made a beeline to her the second they arrived.

Was she using those liver treats she'd clued him in to yesterday? Or was it just her sparkling personality? Probably a little of both, with the bigger share going to her delightful disposition, he was sure.

Soon there was a lull in business, and he spied Molly hustling back toward him, her red curls bouncing against her slim shoulders.

He quickly put his hands on the keyboard and tried to look as if he'd been working away instead of watching her impressive display of sales/doggy advice/customer service skills.

She entered the back room. "How're you coming along?" she asked with a smile.

He nodded a few times. "Good. I'm still checking into some areas of concern," he said, being deliberately vague because he didn't have much else to tell her; he'd found observing her in action so much more fascinating than her computer problem. Not good.

She drew her arched brows together. "Do you think you'll be able to figure things out soon? As I told you earlier, the guy from the IRS is coming in two days, and I still need to organize the files once you figure out where they went."

"Don't worry," he said, waving a hand in the air. "I'll have things under control in plenty of time." He'd just need to buckle down, quit watching her and dig in. He was planning on hitting his own work hard as soon as possible, so buckling down would be good for both of them.

"Oh, good," she said, turning her mouth upward into a relieved-looking smile. "I was worried maybe you were having problems or something."

The only problem he'd had was keeping his attention off her. "Nope, everything is fine. I'm just looking at the problem from all angles. I should have this baby figured out real soon."

The front door buzzer went off. As usual, the dogs jumped up and ran to the door.

Molly turned. "Oh, that's Wanda Fields, here to get the special food I ordered for her cocker spaniel, Zander. I'm just going to head out into the store again and leave you to your work."

She hurried to greet Wanda—a short woman with long dark hair—with a cheery wave and what looked like a welcoming hello. Then she led Wanda to the register, presumably to give her the special food she'd ordered.

Grant dragged his gaze away, determined to live up to his word and figure this computer puzzle out, pronto. Even though focusing on the job instead of the lovely owner was proving to be so much harder than he'd imagined.

Grant finally got up and shut the door, literally blocking his view of the store and its goings-on, as well as Molly. It also served to keep the dogs out in the store so they wouldn't distract him each time they ran to greet every single customer. He then managed to concentrate on his task for a good stretch and started to make progress as he consulted the notes she'd written about the details of the lost files.

Just as he got cooking, he ran into a snag with

her directory. Needing to talk to Molly, he stood, stretched and went looking for her.

He spied her talking with a tall, older man with a cane, handlebar mustache and gray hair. The dapper-looking gent had a plaid tam with a red pom-pom on the top, set at a jaunty angle on his head, and he wore a plaid scarf which matched his tam. Clearly, he was bundled up for the cold December weather.

Just as Grant headed into their aisle, Molly said to the man, "Truly, Neil, I don't mind coming over to install Coco's dog door." Molly turned slightly, and Grant saw that she held a small, fluffy white dog in her arms. "She needs to go out once in a while on her own, don't you, sweetie?" She bent her head and buried her nose in the little dog's neck.

Grant hung back at the end of an aisle, finding himself wondering what that kind of nuzzle would feel like.

"You sure?" Neil asked, his forehead furrowed. "I know you're busy here, and if I could get Hunter Flanigan to come out to put the thing in, I would. But he's booked out a week helping Joe Perkins install new kitchen cabinets, and with my hip and back acting up, I really need the door installed as soon as possible."

"I'm sure," Molly replied with a gentle smile that made Grant's heart squeeze. "Don't you worry, Neil. I'll come over after work and have you set up in no time."

"That'd be great," Neil said.

Grant's impression of Molly rose another notch. Here she was, helping an elderly person in need. She was quite a woman, all right.

Feeling funny about eavesdropping on their conversation, he stepped forward and said, "Excuse me?"

Molly turned. "Hey, Grant. What's up?"

"I need to ask you a few questions."

"Okay, just a second." She put her attention back on Neil, then exclaimed to him, "Oh, have you met Grant Roderick, Rose Latham's nephew?"

"No, I haven't." Neil stepped forward and held out his hand. "Nice to meet you."

Grant shook his hand. "Nice to meet you, too."

"You in town taking care of Jade?" Neil asked, gesturing with his chin to the dog, who was standing on alert at the front door, watching the people go by.

"Well, yes. But Molly here has offered to look after her for a while so I can get some work done."

Neil laughed. "Yeah, that dog's a handful."

"Drove me crazy," Grant admitted.

"So, Neil," Molly said, "do you already have the plywood for the dog door?" she asked.

Neil shook his head. "I have it ordered and paid for, but I haven't been able to pick it up at the hardware store." He grimaced. "I wouldn't be able to get it out of my car."

"I'll pick it up, then, and bring it with me."

"It's pretty big," Neil said, worry lacing his tone.

Grant was thinking the same thing. Molly was just a little bit of a thing. Hardly construction-worker material.

"No problem. I can handle it," Molly said. "You have a jigsaw, right? I'll need one to cut the hole out of the wood for the dog door."

"Sure do. My son left me his when he moved to his apartment in Portland a few years back."

"Good. I'll use that and have you and Coco set up in no time."

"I really appreciate your help, you know. I just can't do things like I used to," Neil said, holding up his cane. "This eighty-year-old body isn't cooperating much anymore."

Molly laid a hand on Neil's arm. "I'm happy to help. I sold you the door so Coco can go out on her own. I want you to be able to use it."

"Well, then, I'll see you later," Neil said. "I'll be home all night, so come on by whenever." He started walking toward the door, limping, leaning on his cane.

"Neil," Molly called, holding up the dog in the air. "Did you forget something?"

Neil turned, then slapped his forehead. "Where is my head?" He limped back and took Coco from Molly's arms. "Sorry, girl," he told the dog while he reversed course to leave. "I would never really forget you."

As soon as Neil had left the store, Molly said to Grant, "He's such a wonderful old man. His wife of sixty years died last year, and he's had a rough time of it. So I've been helping out a bit. With his bad hip and back problems, he's been having difficulty taking Coco out, so he bought a dog door so she can go out on her own."

There was that compassionate woman who impressed Grant so much. And while he really admired her wanting to make Neil's life easier, Grant couldn't help but think that *she* was the one who might need some help with her doggy door installation. Not that she would ever ask for help. Or agree to it easily.

"How big is that piece of plywood you were talking about?" he asked.

"I'm not sure. It's going into a large sliding door glass panel, so pretty big."

He pulled his mouth into a slight frown. "You sure you can handle that by yourself?"

"Pretty sure. The guys at the hardware store can help me tie it onto my car, and I'll manage somehow when I get to Neil's. I'm pretty resourceful."

He'd figured so. But a woman her size muscling a huge sheet of plywood off her car and into Neil's house? No way. And the jigsaw? Those things were tricky machines and, in inexperienced hands, could be dangerous.

"Why don't I help you?" he said before he could stop the words.

She held up her hands and waved them in the air. "Oh, no. That's not necessary."

There was the expected response. Man, she was stubborn. "I think it is." He lifted a brow speculatively. "You have any experience using a jigsaw?"

"Well, no," she conceded.

"I do," he said. "My dad and I did hobby woodworking in our garage when I was growing up. I'm even better at it than he is."

She pursed her lips. "I know you have a deadline to stick to, and you've already helped me here," she said, pointing in the direction of the back room. "I can't ask you to sacrifice any more of your time."

Her point wasn't lost on him. He did have a lot of work ahead of him. A ton, actually. But he'd been raised to help out when necessary—his dad had volunteered a lot of time at church before his mom died—and the thought of Molly struggling to help Neil, all on her own, just didn't sit right with Grant, especially when he had the ability to assist.

"I can't, in good conscience, let you tackle that job on your own. You might hurt yourself," he said.

"To tell you the truth, I was a bit worried about the lifting and jigsawing," Molly said, smoothing her wild hair behind one ear. "I think the piece of plywood is taller than me."

No doubt about it. This wasn't a job for a small woman by herself. "See? There you go. You need to let me help. Working together, I bet we can have that door installed in an hour, tops."

"Are you sure?"

"Positive."

She touched his arm. "That would be great, then."

The warmth of her touch made his skin tingle. "Fantastic." He rubbed his jaw, reeling in his desire to help her today, when he'd already lost so much time working on her computer. "But… could we possibly do it tomorrow night, so I can get some work done?"

"Sure. I think Neil and Coco can wait until then," she said. "I'll call and let him know the change of plans."

Relief eased its way through him. If he played catch-up today, he should be just about where he should be by tomorrow evening. "Good. That'll work better for me."

"Gena is scheduled to work tomorrow evening

and close up, so I'll be off at about six," she said. "Will that work for you?"

"That'll be fine," he said. "Why don't we say we'll meet there at six-thirty tomorrow, all right?"

"Perfect," she replied. "I'll go write Neil's address down. He lives only a couple of blocks from Rose, so you won't have to go far."

She turned and moved to the front desk, and Grant went back to her computer. He sat, realizing he'd veered off course with all their talk of Neil and had forgotten to ask her the questions about her computer system.

He let out a snort. He was obviously having trouble focusing on getting her computer fixed. And on powering through his own work.

What was done was done, though. He'd just buckle down and pull a few all-nighters to make up lost time.

Sounded like a good plan, totally doable.

He hoped so. Because if his case of the Mollys was permanent, a whole lot more than his deadline was toast.

Chapter Six

The next night, Molly drove to Neil's house a half mile from her store to avoid getting blown away by the chilly, windy, yet thankfully dry, weather.

She pulled into Neil's driveway, noticing the twinkling green and red Christmas lights Neil had somehow strung across his small porch. The noble fir she'd helped him cut and decorate last weekend glittered prettily from the front bay window of his quaint cottage-style house, adding to festive holiday air that had taken over Moonlight Cove in the last few days. Christmas was only ten days away and everybody seemed to be getting in the holiday mood.

Noting that Grant hadn't arrived yet—she was a bit early—she sat in her car for a moment, gathering her thoughts. She'd been really busy with the Christmas rush yesterday and today, and she'd been able to keep thoughts of him from clogging her brain pretty well with all the hustle and bustle.

But now, as she sat alone in her car, her day had calmed down significantly, and her brain unwound. And she had no choice but to deal with all of the thoughts of Grant she'd put on the back burner.

Once she let her mind relax, she had to admit that she was deeply touched and impressed that he'd so generously offered to come help her install Neil's dog door. Grant had his own life, his own schedule and tight deadlines, and still he'd insisted on helping out.

For her sake.

He was truly a considerate man. Rose would be proud of her nephew when she returned.

Molly's heart squeezed. While her friends were good friends, and would certainly help her if she asked for it, she didn't ask much, and was used to being the one helping out, not the other way around. So it had thrown her a bit when Grant had offered to assist.

Despite her surprise, she'd managed to deal with his offer, and had accepted because she wasn't an idiot; she'd probably need his muscle, and jigsaw experience, to do the job right. No sense in ignoring her practical side. Helping Neil was her ultimate goal—what did it matter how she accomplished that? Even if Grant was involved.

Good question. One tempered with the nagging thought that it wasn't such a good idea to be spending so much time with a man who kept proving to her, over and over again, that he was a really good guy. One she actually liked.

But liking him meant nothing. It just wouldn't do for her to fall for any man. She found love for other people, but not for herself. Never herself. Just the thought of dating again made her want to hyperventilate.

Her heart skipping, she leaned over and put her forehead on the cool steering wheel, shaking her head slightly, calling upon her common sense, inner calm and faith to settle her down.

The fact was, she needed to ignore how much Grant's kindness and consideration appealed to her and focus on helping Neil. Then she and Grant would go their separate ways and her life would get back to normal.

She straightened, tapping her fingers against her legs. From now on she would make a concerted effort to not only stay away from him, but to set him up with someone else as she'd promised Rose. Quickly. And Molly would watch from afar. Very far if she were smart.

Lord, help me be strong. Help me do the right thing, always.

Feeling better, she perked up when she noticed Grant's Bug pulling into the driveway next to her. She did a double take when he pulled closer and she saw that he had a giant piece of plywood tied to the roof of his car.

They'd agreed when they parted yesterday to come double-check the measurements for the wood and go pick it up together, using her small but practical SUV to transport it. Guess he'd changed his mind. How the thing had stayed on for the three-block trip from the hardware store was anybody's guess. But it had.

She got out of her car and flipped the hood of her jacket up as a blast of wind hit her.

Grant met her in between the two vehicles.

"I thought we were going to get the plywood together," she said loudly to be heard over the gusting wind. "I have a roof rack, remember?"

"I know," he replied. "But I didn't want you messing with this." He gestured to the wood.

She endured more heart squeezing. Oh, my. How considerate was that? "Are you sure it's the right size?"

"I came by earlier and Neil was happy to let me measure the window."

Her jaw loosened. When he said he was going

to help, he meant it. She liked that. More than she should. "You did that for me?"

"Yup." He began to untie the piece of wood balanced precariously on top of his car. "I'm proactive."

She furrowed her brow as she began to help him. "Did you get any of your own stuff done?"

Shrugging, he said, "Some." He got the knot undone, and then put one hand on the wood to hold it in place. "But I'm a night owl, so I can pull all-nighters if I have to."

The very idea of going a night without sleep horrified her, but she remembered her dad often worked through the night when he had a big case, holed up in his home office in the basement, essentially unavailable. Even when her father was there, at home, she'd been alone.

"I'd be a wreck the next day if I stayed up all night," she said. Her dad had been just plain crabby. "I'm an eight-hour-a-night girl for sure."

"Sleep is a luxury when I'm on deadline," Grant said, then gestured with his chin to the passenger side of the car. "Would you mind going over there to open the door so I can get the rope out?"

"Got it." She did as he asked, thinking on her way to the other side of the car that Grant was even more like her dad than she'd thought.

Definitely not her type. If she had one anymore.

She put a hand on the wood to hold it in place as Grant loosened the rope and pulled it off.

He eyed her gloved hand. "You sure you should be doing this with your cut?"

"It's fine," she said, waving her injured hand in the air as she tried not to let his concern impress or affect her too much. "I wore my thick gloves to protect it."

"Let me know if it hurts you, all right?"

"Promise."

Together they lifted the awkward piece of wood off the car and carried it up the driveway and the path leading to the covered porch. The wind had Molly's coat hood flopping down over her eyes and she had to hold her head at an odd angle to see where she was going.

As they went up the concrete stairs, Grant carried the bulk of the weight, and Molly realized that she would have never been able to wrangle this piece of wood into Neil's house by herself.

Good thing for Neil, she'd agreed to let Grant help. Good thing Grant had offered.

Just as they set the wood down and Molly flung her annoying hood off her head, Coco started barking in the house, announcing their arrival.

A moment later, the inner door rattled and Neil opened it, and Coco—a Maltese—greeted them from her owner's arms with a yip. Christmas music—Doris Day singing "Silver Bells," one of Molly's mom's favorites—wafted out onto the porch. A pang of old grief shuddered through Molly's heart, but she did her best to ignore it for the time being.

"Hey, you two," Neil said, waving. "Glad to see you made it here with the plywood."

"Grant tied it to the top of his Bug," Molly said with what she hoped was an upbeat grin, shoving her sadness down. "I can't believe it stayed on in all this wind."

Neil nodded. "He's a real good problem solver." He smiled at Molly, his eyes twinkling. "A nice young man, too, don't you think? Quite the catch for a pretty gal like you."

Molly blinked, Neil's message coming through loud and clear. Not surprising since it was evident he wasn't the least bit interested in being subtle.

Had everyone she knew in Moonlight Cove turned into a matchmaker? Well, matchmaking was her turf, and she wasn't going to give it up, especially when all of the other so-called matchmakers—Phoebe and Neil, for starters— had their eyes on setting Molly up with Grant. Being designated as the town's unofficial matchmaker had its advantages—such as avoiding any setups by virtue of being the one doing the setting up.

Good way to keep her heart safe and unscathed, wasn't it?

"Whatever you say," Molly replied, hoping to gloss over Neil's loaded question about Grant being a good catch.

"So does that mean you'll go out with him?" Neil asked, skewering her with a pointed gaze.

Her cheeks heated, and she was glad for the nip of the winter wind coming off the ocean. Talk about direct. "Now, Neil, you know I only set people up on dates and that I don't go on any dates myself." She gestured to Grant and widened her eyes, imploring him to help her out. "And Grant knows that, too."

Grant got the gist and chimed in. "Actually, I don't date, either, Neil, so I'm afraid your efforts to get us together are in vain."

Neil scoffed. "Now, see, I think you two are just being foolish. I had sixty years with my Irma, and I wouldn't trade one second of that time for anything. If you ask me, love's a wonderful thing."

Except when it hurt, which in Molly's experience was all the time. She arched a sly brow. "Then why don't I set you up with someone nice, Neil? There are plenty of eligible ladies your age here in town." If she turned the discussion around, maybe she could get Neil to back off.

"Oh, I'm too old to be dating like some sixty-year-old whippersnapper," Neil said with a slow shake of his head. "But you two are young, and you should both have someone to share your lives with." He pondered Grant. "This little gal here is the nicest person you could ever hope to meet, always putting others first. You could do a lot worse, you know."

Molly sent a brief yet pleading glance Grant's way.

"Neil, I hate to break it to you, but I'm only going to be here a few weeks, until Aunt Rose and Benny get back, and I'm going to be working the whole time, so it isn't really practical for me to be dating," Grant said politely but firmly. "Why don't we just stick with getting this doggy door in, all right?"

Neil pushed the storm door out, then propped it open. "Of course, of course. But I still think you two should at least spend some time getting to know each other. No better way to fall in love, if you ask me."

A chill sliced through Molly, and it had nothing to do with the cold December weather and everything to do with the fact that, unfortunately, what Neil had said was exactly what she was most afraid of.

Grant looked at Molly, noticing her furrowed brow. Looked like all this talk of dating bothered her as much as it did him. At least they were on the same page; no matter how wonderful Molly was proving to be, he had no intention of pursuing a romance. He barely had time for his work now as it was. For so many reasons, dating Molly, or anybody, was simply not going to happen.

Even so, he was glad he'd insisted on helping her with this job; she and Neil would never have been able to manage on their own. And, actually, it felt good to be taking a break from work.

Eager to get to work—and direct Neil's attention away from trying to shove Molly and him together—he rubbed his hands in front of him. "Can you hold the door open for us?" he asked Neil, redirecting the conversation to the task at hand. "I want to be sure it's going to fit, and then we can take it out to the garage to cut the hole for the door."

"Sure can." Neil backed up and put Coco down out of the way. "Stay, girl," he said. She obediently sat, her black eyes watching their every move. "Good dog." Neil then stepped forward and held the inner wooden door open wide. "Bring 'er in."

In tandem, Molly and Grant lifted the wood and carried it to Neil's bedroom at the back of the house where they were going to install it in a glass sliding door. Neil followed behind, and so did Coco, her toenails clicking on the hardwood floor.

Molly was stronger than she looked and handled the hefty piece of plywood well for a petite woman.

As they carried the board through the house, Grant noticed a lovely traditionally decorated living area to his left, graced with a huge Christmas tree, plaid couches and a fireplace with a nice fire crackling away. And to his surprise, the biggest state-of-the-art flat-screen TV he'd ever seen sitting on an enormous entertainment center jammed on one wall.

"Wow, nice TV," he said, pausing for a moment to admire the spectacular piece of electronic equipment. "That's the biggest one I've ever seen."

Neil flushed, looking a bit embarrassed. "Yeah, I know it's pretty over-the-top," he admitted. "But watching sports on TV is my one guilty pleasure, so I splurged a bit on the setup." His face brightened. "Hey, the Seahawks play the Steelers on Monday night. You interested in watching with me and Molly? It's gonna be a great game."

Grant set down his side of the wood on the carpeted floor, then looked inquiringly at Molly as she set down her side, her lips pressed together tightly. "You a football fan?" he asked her.

She flexed her hand. "I watch sometimes, mostly with Neil." Lowering her voice so only Grant could hear, she whispered, "He likes the company."

Grant nodded, once again impressed by the redhead standing next to him. "Ah. I see." And he did see—that Molly once again was proving to him that she was a really great person who often put others first. Like it or not, he admired that trait.

"So, what do you say?" Neil asked, gesturing to the jumbotron in his living room, his face wreathed in what looked like eager anticipation. "I'm making my famous chili to serve at halftime."

Oh, man. Football and chili. It didn't get any better than that. Tempting…

Grant reeled in his desire to give in and agree to come watch the game. His deadline loomed, and he'd already lost a lot of time yesterday and today helping Molly and Neil. As soon as he finished this project, he really needed to keep outside activities to a minimum. As in, all work, all the time, no exceptions.

But he didn't have the heart to disappoint Neil. So instead, he said, "I'll have to see how my work goes. Maybe I can squeeze it in."

Neil smiled. "I hope you can. It's going to be a fun night, isn't it, Moll?"

She returned his smile, sort of, though the lifting of her lips looked a little forced. "It always is," she replied. "But you know, Grant is here in Moonlight Cove to get a lot of work done, so, as he said, it's going to be difficult for him to find the time."

It sounded like she didn't want him to horn in on watching the game, and, oddly, that rankled a bit. Was she that eager to get rid of him?

And, more important, why did he care? He should be happy she was backing him up. So why wasn't he?

"I know, I know," Neil said before Grant could figure out his conflicting feelings. "But he can't work every minute of the day. Surely he's going to want to take a break."

Not if Grant could help it. "I'll have to play it by ear," he said to temporarily placate Neil. "I'll let you know, all right?"

Neil nodded.

Good. Grant put his hands on the wood. "You ready to get moving?" he asked Molly. Time to get on track so he could get back to work. Eventually. The way things were going, he'd never meet his deadline.

"Let's do this," she replied, picking up her end.

Once in the master bedroom, which was graced by what looked to Grant's untrained eye to be an impressive collection of mahogany antique furniture, they went to work measuring the window with the tape measure Neil supplied.

Grant had been taught to measure at least twice,

cut once, so he double-checked his numbers with the tape measure Neil had provided.

"Looks like we're right on," he said, trying hard to ignore the fresh smell of Molly's hair floating around him as they measured together, marking the position of the hole they were going to cut out of the wood for the dog door.

Once Neil left to fix his dinner, Coco lingered and got herself involved, begging for petting every time Molly bent down to hold the tape measure. She giggled as Coco tried to nose her way under Molly's hand, and the sound of her laughter made Grant smile.

He shoved the tape measure into his jeans pocket. "Should we take the plunge and make our cuts?" he asked Molly when he was satisfied they had the measurements right.

She pushed her hair back from her face and gave him a thumbs-up. "I think we're ready."

Soon they had the wood laying across two sawhorses in Neil's garage, with the jigsaw Neil's son had left nearby. They were ready to rock.

Neil appeared in the doorway that led to the kitchen, his cane in his hand, his gray eyebrows raised. "Do you two mind if I stay inside while you make quick work of that wood?" He gestured to his left side. "The cold out here makes my hip act up."

"Go sit down by the fire and relax," Grant said before Molly could respond. "We've got this under control."

Neil pointed to a box with some tools in it. "I gathered up the stuff you might need. Let me know if something's missing."

"Will do," Grant said, casting his gaze over the assortment of tools in the box, noting a level, screwdriver and an assortment of pencils.

Neil pointed to the garage's far wall. "There's the door."

Grant saw the dog door propped against the wall, still packed in the box. "Oh, great."

With a wave, Neil left, and Grant and Molly unpacked the dog door.

"It's pretty small," he said when they had it out.

"Coco's tiny," she replied with a smile. "She doesn't need a big door. Besides, I wanted the door small enough to discourage other animals from coming in."

He raised his brows. "Other animals?"

"Asbolutely," she said. "My neighbor woke up one morning and found a raccoon in his kitchen that had come in through the dog door." She chuckled. "Almost gave the poor man a heart attack."

"Well, we don't want that, now, do we?" he said.

"Definitely not."

He went over to the box, grabbed a pencil,

shoved it behind his ear, then pulled the tape measure out of his pocket.

"Let's measure this baby."

Together they marked off the door's dimensions, then went to work figuring out where the cuts would need to be made on the wood.

As he was doing the calculations, Molly asked, "Did you and your dad work together like this a lot?"

He nodded. "Yup. Dad loved building stuff out of wood. We'd spend hours on the weekends making things."

"What did you build?" she asked, her voice sounding kind of wistful.

He handed her the end of the tape. "We started with birdhouses, then worked up to wooden toys and then garden benches. The last thing we made together before I left for college was a beautiful cherry cradle."

"Oh, that sounds lovely."

"It is." He made a tick mark on the wood. "My dad still has it, stored away in the attic. He's saving it for his grandchildren."

"You think you'll have kids?" she asked softly.

Her question stilled his hands, and a dart of regret found its target. "Probably not."

"Why?"

He adjusted the tape measure and made another mark. "I just don't see a wife and kids in my future." No sense in not being honest. There was no room in his life for any kind of family, save his dad. Though the space in his chest that had filled with warmth and contentment the night he and Molly had made dinner in Rose's kitchen pulsed again.

She was quiet for a moment. "I love kids," she finally said. "I actually thought I might adopt one or two down the line."

Surprised, he looked up at Molly to see if she was serious. Her solemn expression told him she was. "You'd want to be a single parent?"

"I'd consider it," she said. "There are lots of older kids who need good homes."

The warmth spread through his chest. Seemed she was always taking those in need under her wing. "True. But single parenting? That'd be rough," he said with a quick shake of his head.

"Hey, I grew up in a single-parent household, remember," she said with a lift of her chin. "I know what it's like."

He gave his head a mental slap; he should really think before he spoke. "I know," he said, putting the pencil back behind his ear. "I'm sorry. That was an insensitive thing to say."

"No, no, you're right. But see, I know from experience how much someone can help a child in need." She looked away, her mouth turned down in a small frown. "I would have given anything when I was growing up to have someone step in and take care of me."

Protectiveness roared through him. "Did your dad abuse you?" he asked, staring intently at her. "Because if he did…" He wasn't usually prone to violence, but in this instance, he could be convinced.

She shook her head. "Not physically, no, and I always had a roof over my head, clothes to wear and enough food to eat. But he neglected me emotionally when my mom died, and I was so lonely at times, I wondered how I'd make it to the next day." She looked right at him. "Do you know, my dad never set foot in any of my schools? He never came to any of my graduations, either."

Another surge of protectiveness lurched through Grant. Resisting the crazy urge to take her in his arms, he said, "Wow, that must have been really hard." His mom and dad had been there through all of his sporting events, choir concerts and school conferences.

"It *was* hard," she said, her jaw firm. "So imagine how hard it would be for a kid who doesn't have a mother *or* a father. It would be unbearable."

"You're right," he said, admiring her desire to spare other kids what she'd been through. She was really something. "I guess coming from a loving two-parent home has skewed my view of the world some."

"Probably," she said. "I'm just glad you had a happy childhood. I envy you that, you know. You were very lucky."

He'd never really thought about that before. "You're right," he said. "I guess I've taken my happy childhood for granted." Odd how that made him feel a bit guilty, even though he was sure that hadn't been her intention. She didn't seem like the type to shove guilt onto anybody. Quite the opposite, in fact.

"I think a lot of people take happiness for granted. But I don't," she said. "If I can spare some child even one-tenth of the unhappiness I went through, then I will."

"You have an amazing attitude about the whole thing," he said. Once again, she impressed him.

"Why do you say that?" she asked.

He clicked the tape measure closed. "A lot of people would be bitter about a rough childhood. You're not."

"Oh, trust me, I have moments of bitterness," she said, putting her hands in her jeans pockets. "But I have to learn from my dad's mistakes and trust that God has a plan for me."

"Which is?" he asked, more curious than he should be about what made her tick.

"Helping others find love."

"I guess that makes sense," he said, yet he was uneasy with her talk about trusting a God who had betrayed him. "So you're saying you trust in God's plan?"

"Of course." She blinked. "Don't you?"

He studied the marks he'd made on the board, wondering how much he should share with her. He looked up and saw her gazing at him, her eyes full of compassion, and decided confiding in her wasn't a big deal. "I'm not sure I do."

"Really? Why not?"

He erased a mark and started to remeasure. "Because his plan for my mom took her away from a family who loved her."

Molly was silent for a long moment, then she reached out and touched his arm and gently squeezed. "Sometimes God's plan seems cruel, doesn't it?"

"You've got that right," he said, straightening, liking her comforting touch just a little too much. "What kind of merciful God does something like that?"

"I don't know how to answer that, but God does," she said, her eyes softening. "Have you prayed about this?"

He tightened his jaw. "I haven't prayed or set foot in a church since the day my mom died."

Her eyes grew wide. "Oh, wow. You've really lost faith, haven't you?"

All he could do was nod.

She moved a bit closer. "You want to talk about it?"

His earlier unease came rushing back. What in the world was he doing, discussing this with Molly? Some things were just too painful to share, and the wound he'd suffered when his mom died was still tender to the touch. A part of him believed it would never heal completely; why poke at the injury?

"Actually, I'd rather we just got back to work," he said, taking the smart, safe road. The one leading away from having any kind of heart-to-heart with Molly.

The one he had to keep himself on.

"You sure?" she asked, her voice soft, and very, very compelling. "I'm a good listener."

He looked at her again, standing there, ready to give him all the help he needed. Good thing he didn't need any. "Positive," he replied. "Thanks, anyway."

"You're welcome," she said. "If you change your mind, you know where to find me, right?"

"Right," he said automatically, even though after he finished fixing her computer, finding her should be the last thing on his mind.

He'd have to make sure of it if he had any hope of meeting his deadline.

Why did that suddenly seem easier said than done?

Chapter Seven

An hour later, Molly stepped back to admire the doggy door she and Grant had successfully installed.

She gave Grant a high five. "Looks great," she said. "This is going to be so much easier for Neil."

Grant grinned. "We're a good team, aren't we?"

Unexpectedly, her heart squeezed; they would never be a true team. "I didn't do much," she said lightly, trying to belie the inexplicable sadness creeping through her. "In reality, I wouldn't have been able to do this without your help."

"I have a feeling you would have found a way," he replied, picking up the tools they'd used. "You seem pretty resourceful to me."

"Well, I try to be, but the jigsaw was trickier to use than I expected." Although having Grant instruct her on the tool's use had been fun. Especially the part where he'd guided her hands around a tight corner cut. In her dreams, he could be her teacher any day.

She reeled back such thoughts. In real life, though, she probably enjoyed working with Grant—and being close to him—just a little too much for a woman bent on avoiding attachment to any man. This project had been a one-time thing, clearly too dangerous to repeat. And any kind of teamwork would be a thing of the past. She'd have to be content having God as her only teammate.

Sobering, she followed Grant out of the room and down the hall. When they entered the kitchen, they found Neil hunched over the kitchen sink with a plunger in his hands.

Grant rushed forward. "Hey, there, Neil. What's the problem?"

Neil turned, his face slightly red from exertion. "Oh, my garbage disposal is clogged up again."

"Let me have a look," Grant said, putting the tools in his hands on the tile kitchen counter. "You shouldn't be doing this with your bad hip."

Neil stepped to the side, and Grant took over using the plunger, putting his muscular arms and chest into the task of clearing the clog.

Impressive. Molly tried not to stare.

After a few plunges, he turned, grimacing. "Stubborn one, isn't it?"

"Yup," Neil replied. "I oughta know better than to put too many eggshells down there."

Grant gave Neil a wry smile. "Eggshells'll get you every time."

Grant kept at the task, and as Molly watched him work, her chest tightened. Even with his own deadline looming, Grant was concerned for Neil, and had taken even more time to help the older man. A small thing, yes, but considerate just the same.

She liked that. A lot.

It took only a few more minutes for Grant to get the drain clear. As soon as he had the disposal running correctly, he shook the plunger off and raised it in the air. "Victory!" he exclaimed with a hearty grin. "This drain is clear."

Molly grinned. She'd seen Grant smile, sure. But she hadn't seen him *smile*.

"Thank goodness," Neil said, reaching for the plunger. "Don't know what I would have done without you two."

Molly patted his arm. "Well, you won't have to find out, will you?"

"Well, seeing as how this one here won't be in town long," Neil said, nodding toward Grant, "I hope you and I, Molly-girl, can figure all of these problems out on our own."

That reality check of a statement brought Molly down to earth. "Oh, we'll do just fine on our own," she managed to say, quite breezily, in fact. Here she was, all impressed with Grant, despite her best efforts to stay on an even keel, and the truth of the matter was, Grant wasn't going to be hanging around Moonlight Cove for long.

Another reason, among many, she had to stay immune to his myriad charms.

"I'm sure you won't even miss me," Grant said as he washed his hands and dried them with one of the paper towels on the roll next to the sink.

Molly forced a smile, but remained silent. She wasn't touching that one with a ten-foot plunger.

Neil chimed in instead. "Well, I, for one, will." He bent down and picked Coco up. "All the more reason you should come to watch the football game on TV next Monday with me and Molly and Coco here."

Grant gave Neil an indulgent smile, his eyes crinkling appealingly at the corners. "Like I said, I'll have to play that by ear, but I'll do my best to try to make an appearance, all right?"

Neil harrumphed. "Guess I'll have to be happy with that."

Grant clapped him on the shoulder but didn't reply. Seemed as if he didn't want to get Neil's hopes up too far. Molly needed to do the same with herself.

Molly and Grant gathered up their coats and said goodbye, both refusing the older man's offer of dinner; it was getting late.

All bundled up, she and Grant headed outside

to their cars. A stiff breeze still blew, and the temperature had dropped as the evening had worn on.

They reached Molly's car first. She turned to Grant, flipping her coat's collar up against the cold. "Thank you so much for all of your help. I know you gave up a lot of your own time to help Neil."

"He reminds me a bit of my dad," Grant replied with a small grin, shoving his hands into his coat pockets. "It just didn't seem right leaving him and Coco high and dry."

Molly's heart warmed, creating a cozy, comfortable glow in her chest she could get used to, but wouldn't. "Well, I appreciate your time, and I know Neil does, too."

"No problem. I actually enjoyed the dog door project. It's been a while since I've done any woodworking."

"Too busy, right?" she said with a lift of her brow.

"Pretty much," he admitted. "My work doesn't leave a lot of time for hobbies."

Sounded sadly familiar. Her dad's hobby had been…well, nothing. Unfortunately, work had ruled his life. "Maybe you ought to take some time out once in a while to do things you enjoy."

"Sounds easy," Grant said with a rueful grin. "But in my business, no one gets ahead by taking a lot of time off."

"And getting ahead is important to you, right?" she asked, just to be sure she had him straight, although why that mattered was anybody's guess.

"It's everything."

Those two words had the warm glow in her chest going dark and chilly. "Why?" she asked before she could call the word back. Oh, well. Maybe she needed to hear the answer so the glow in her heart would stay extinguished.

He paused, his brow furrowed. "I'm not sure," he said, looking off into the distance for a moment, his brain obviously spinning. "Being successful in my career is important to me, always has been. I never want to go back to being the nerdy kid with the pocket protector."

Surprise bounced through her. "I can't believe that was ever you," she said, even though Rose had described him as such. A guy full of quirky information? Check. A techie? Check. A bit of a computer geek? Well, yeah. But true nerd? Not even close. "A lot of words come to mind when I think of you, but *nerd* isn't one of them."

He leaned against her car and gazed at her speculatively. "So what words come to mind, then?"

Kind. Giving. Handsome. Not that she could tell him that. At least not the *handsome* part.

"Well…let's see." She tapped her lips. "Helpful. Kind. Generous…" Distracting. Fascinating. *Dangerous.*

"Those all sound great," he said, grinning. "Looks like I've made a good impression."

"…too involved in work, driven, overly focused." He cringed. "Ouch."

"Hey, you asked," she said, shrugging. "I call 'em like I see 'em." And what she saw was that Grant was too much like her father for comfort. Not something she was going to ignore.

"And I expect no less," Grant told her. "Speaking of work…" He pointed to his car. "I've got to get to it."

Of course he did. Funny, though, how she wished they could stand there and continue talking. Or better yet, go back to her place where it was warm and talk until the middle of the night.

Shoving such outlandish thoughts to the back of her mind, she said, "Well, I guess I'll see you first thing in the morning, right? Around eight?"

He rounded the front of her car on the way to his, then opened his car door. "Right. I should have your problem fixed in plenty of time for your appointment with the tax man."

"Okay, great," she said, waving. Rather than stand there and stare at him, she dug out her keys and got in her car.

With a toot of his horn, he slowly backed out of the driveway and drove away.

Molly watched his taillights disappear down the road, her thoughts chaotic. On the one hand, she was glad she'd been reminded how much Grant was like her dad. She needed that reality to re-inforce that no matter how much she might be charmed by Grant, she had to keep her guard up to protect her heart.

Sounded simple. And she should be an expert in that particular endeavor, right?

Right.

But as she sat there in the dark, with the wind blowing around and nothing but Neil's twinkling Christmas lights illuminating her car, she couldn't help but remember how much she'd enjoyed work-ing with Grant today. And his smile had made her melt.

She huffed out a breath. What was it about a man who knew his way around home improve-ment projects, anyway? She could get used to watching Grant wield a power tool mighty quick, not to mention how touched she'd been when he refused to leave until he'd unclogged Neil's kitchen sink.

With all that in mind, she pondered what Grant had said about her not missing him when he left town. He was dead wrong.

Because she was very, very afraid that she was going to miss him much more than a woman out to safeguard her heart should.

Bowing her head, she sent a prayer for strength straight to God's ear.

* * *

The next day, after pulling an all-nighter hunched over his computer, Grant walked with Jade to Molly's store, hoping the brisk morning air would wake him up a bit.

The leaden gray clouds had partially cleared out, leaving dull patches of blue to peek through the wispy clouds remaining. All in all, it was a beautiful, if chilly, December morning in Moonlight Cove. He'd have to enjoy this weather while he could; no doubt the usual coastal rain would start up again soon enough.

He took a few deep breaths as he walked toward Main Street, filling his lungs with the fresh ocean air, clearing the cobwebs from his head caused by lack of sleep. With a clear head came thoughts of Molly.

Just peachy.

Deep down, he couldn't help but admit that he really liked spending time with her. She was funny, warm-hearted and really down-to-earth, all qualities that appealed to him. Her concern for her friends especially drew him in, and had him sacrificing precious work time to help others. Crazy, but there it was.

While on the one hand, he really liked helping out, on the other hand, he really couldn't afford the time away from his own work. He talked a good story to Molly about staying up all night not bothering him, but the truth of it was he really couldn't get by having too many nights without some shut-eye.

So he was going to have to make a concerted effort to stay on his work schedule from now on. Getting caught up in Molly and all of her pet projects just wasn't a good idea if he was going to have any hope of meeting his deadline without frying his brain through lack of sleep.

Life was about choices, and work was his. He'd made the choice, and he was sticking to it. He had to remember that when he was tempted to help out Molly and all of her friends. Even though her endeavor to assist others was noble and admirable, he couldn't make her life his own. Absolutely not.

Jade snarfed, as if her poodle opinion of his choice differed greatly.

"Fine." He hadn't asked for her opinion.

Jade's tail nevertheless started going a mile a minute, and she pulled heavily on the leash. Of course, they were two blocks from Molly's store; she obviously knew that playtime with her two best friends was at hand.

But, he ruthlessly reminded himself, this time with Molly was not a social hour for him; he needed to get in, finish up with fixing her computer and get out. Period. He had a mountain of work waiting for him back at Aunt Rose's.

A few minutes later, he arrived at Bow Wow

Boutique feeling more alert and on track now that the cold and invigorating walk had jump-started him.

He tried the door, but it was locked; made sense because the store didn't open for another two hours. He knocked softly and immediately heard barking. A second later, Peter and Parker came bounding to the door, Molly following quickly behind them.

Grant's heart did a funny lurch when he saw Molly through the front window; she looked really good today in a festive green sweater and slim jeans tucked into flat black boots. She had some of her hair pulled up off her face with a clip thingy, and the style really highlighted her delicate bone structure and auburn brows.

As she opened the door, smiling, he couldn't help but notice how well the green sweater complemented her eyes. If he didn't watch himself, he could drown in those pretty pools of emerald green.

Good thing he was in the know about letting Molly's attractiveness get to him, wasn't it? As long as he continued to be vigilant about not allowing her charm to affect him, he'd be just fine.

As soon as the thought crossed his mind, Jade's leash suddenly went taut; too late he realized the rambunctious dog had bolted into the store to get to Peter and Parker. Pulled off balance, he quickly let the leash go and awkwardly righted himself just in time to keep from face-planting in front of Molly for the second time.

As Jade took off down the main aisle of the store, Peter and Parker yipping happily as they chased her, Grant felt his cheeks go hot, though he tried to act as if he hadn't almost crashed and burned again.

Nice work, bud. If he didn't get a hold of himself—and his wayward preoccupation with Molly—she'd soon think he was the clumsiest man in Moonlight Cove. If not the world.

Molly giggled. "Wow. Guess she's glad to be here."

So am I.

Another rogue thought; this one brought Grant up short, and he fumbled with his reply for a second. "Um…yeah." He held up his right hand and shook it in the air. "She almost yanked my arm off trying to get here faster."

A frown formed between Molly's eyebrows. "If her pulling is becoming a problem, we could always put her in a head collar," she said. "They work really well on dogs that pull."

"I don't think we'll have to change her lead," Grant said, keeping to himself that his being so preoccupied with Molly was the problem, not Jade's pulling; if he hadn't been staring at Molly, he would have seen Jade's lunge in enough time to counter its effectiveness.

Yet another good reason to keep his fascination with the lovely Miss Kent under control. The way things were going, he'd be in traction with a dislocated shoulder, wrenched back, scraped face and bruised pride within hours.

"Oh, okay, well...let me know if you change your mind."

"Sure will," he replied, glad she hadn't mentioned his annoying propensity for falling down—or nearly so—in front of her.

She stepped closer, peering at him, and her fresh, flowery scent washed over him. "You don't look so good."

He ran a hand through his hair self-consciously and fought the urge to move back, away from her alluring scent, into safer territory. "I don't?"

"No. You have dark circles under your eyes."

"Not closing them does tend to cause dark circles, yes," he admitted.

Pursing her lips, she said, "Why don't we skip this, then, so you can get some rest?"

He held up his hands. "Absolutely not," he replied. "I told you I'd fix your problem, and I'm not going back on my word."

"Maybe I can reschedule."

"No, you don't reschedule the IRS, trust me."

"Yeah, I guess you're right." She turned worried eyes to him. "But I still feel bad for taking you away from your work."

"Don't worry, I'm used to working under pressure. I can handle a couple days short on sleep."

"If you're sure…?"

"I am," he said. It wasn't her problem he'd overcommitted.

She nodded, then grabbed her coat off the hook in back of the counter. "Okay, I'm suddenly starving, so I'm going to go to the Coffee Cabana down the street for coffee and something to eat. You want anything?"

His stomach growled at the mention of food. "Actually, yeah, a coffee and muffin sounds great. I'm going to need all the caffeine and sugar I can get this morning." He still had a long day of work ahead of him, with sleep nowhere on the horizon.

She put her coat on, then pulled her curls out from underneath her collar. "I'll have them make it extra strong just for you."

"Thanks," he said, trying not to follow her too closely with his much-too-interested gaze.

"Why don't you get started, and I'll be back in no time with your breakfast and coffee, extra strong." She stopped at the door and turned, hitting him with those gorgeous green eyes. "How does a blueberry scone sound?"

"Perfect," he said, managing to sound normal,

even though he felt like a teenager crushing on the girl next door.

"I'll be back in a few," she said. "And be sure and unhook Jade's leash. It's dangerous for her to be running around with it on." Then she was out the door and gone, nothing but the scent of her fresh perfume lingering behind.

All three dogs ran to the door as it closed. Grant made a grab for Jade and stopped her long enough to unhook the leash. Then the canine trio took off again toward the back of the store, twelve paws skidding on the floor, presumably to attack the huge toy bin Molly had back there.

Grant chuckled at their antics as he headed to the back room to get to work fixing Molly's computer. Focusing on the problem at hand rather than on Molly was the key. He knew that. Now he just had to ignore how charming he found her and power through.

Just as her computer booted up, he heard a knock on the door out front. The dogs went nuts and ran out to see who was there to visit them. It was a dog store, after all; in their minds, chances were probably pretty good they had another canine visitor.

He tilted his chair back to get a clear view of the front window and saw Phoebe standing there wearing a red knit hat, puffy white jacket and jeans.

Her eyes formed large O's, and then she slowly smiled and waved at him by flicking her fingers in the air.

Unease shot through him; her smile seemed… odd. Scheming, even.

He waved back, a single snap of his wrist, hoping she'd move on. He didn't have a lot of time to spare.

No such luck. She motioned to the door handle. Obviously, she wanted in.

Sighing—great, another distraction to deal with—he stood and headed over to the door, grabbing some doggy treats on the way by the front counter. An apt pupil, he asked all three dogs to sit.

To his amazement, they sat, and he treated them. Good; the last thing he needed was to chase runaway dogs all over town. Plus, Molly would never forgive him if he let one of her babies out. Neither would his aunt.

Satisfied the dogs would stay put momentarily, he opened the door a crack, making sure they couldn't bolt if something particularly thrilling happened outside. Whatever that might be.

Phoebe said, "Hi, Grant." She raised her eyebrows, then craned her head to look around him. "Is Molly here?"

He shook his head. "Nope. She went to get coffee."

"Oh, good. Because I want to talk to you."

Brought up short by her words, he blinked, but didn't move. Wariness bubbled inside of him. Why would she want to talk to him? She barely knew him.

After a few seconds, she said, "Can I come in? It's kind of cold out here." She puffed air out from her lips. "I can see my breath."

Resigned that he'd have to talk for a few minutes, he hesitantly moved back and gestured her in. "Of course, come in."

She moved past him, unwinding her scarf as the dogs forgot about sitting and danced around her feet.

He shut the door and followed her in. "What's up?"

Off came her hat, freeing her blond curls. She squatted down to pet the pups. "I need to talk to you about Molly."

His neck heated. "What about her?"

Phoebe rose, and the dogs took off toward the back of the store again, presumably to see if any new toys had appeared since they'd checked the toy basket three minutes ago.

"Well, now you know she's the resident matchmaker around here, right?" Phoebe said.

Nodding, he leaned against the counter. "Uh-huh." Where was this leading?

"And you also know that she wants to fix you up with me."

"And I told her I didn't want to be fixed up with anybody."

"Doesn't matter," Phoebe said emphatically, putting her hat on the counter.

"What do you mean?"

"I mean that when Molly sets her matchmaking sights on someone, nothing will stop her from doing her thing." Phoebe smiled grimly, shaking her head. "She's pretty stubborn."

"I'm pretty stubborn myself." Especially when it came to dating and romance. Definitely ruthless in that department. For his career, he had to be. "I can stop her."

"Oh, braver, stronger men have tried and lost," Phoebe said, waving an emphatic finger in the air. "She wore longtime bachelor holdout Earl Hinman down until he finally relented and went out with Rebecca Blake just to get Molly to leave him alone."

"What happened?" Grant asked, almost afraid to hear her answer.

"They eloped a month later," Phoebe said, deadpan.

Grant pulled in his chin. "Oh. Wow." Just what he needed—a stubborn matchmaker hounding him day and night.

"I'm telling you, she's relentless." Phoebe unzipped her coat. "Even though you told her to back off, she called me late last night making noises about you and I going out this week."

"Not good," he said, shaking his head. He knew Molly was mule-headed, but this…this dogged determination of hers was a distraction he just didn't need.

"No, it's not good," Phoebe replied. Her eyes brightened. "But I think I have a way to get her to stop."

"Let's hear it," Grant said, eager to get Molly off the matchmaker bandwagon so he could relax and get back to business as usual.

"We let her set us up, we go out, we announce we're incompatible and that's that." She snapped her fingers. "Easy."

He raised a brow. "You think it'll work?"

"Pretty sure," Phoebe said with a half nod. "And, really, how can she argue with us after we've agreed to a date?"

"She can't, I guess," he said, cocking his head. Ingenious, really. But would Phoebe's plan work? Molly seemed pretty determined.

"Exactly," Phoebe proclaimed, pointing at him.

He paused, letting her suggestion sink in. "I don't know…" Oddly, a part of him didn't like Molly thinking he was interested in Phoebe. Why, though?

He chewed on his cheek. Did he really want to delve deep enough to answer that question? His bottom line was work and always had been. Not a cute little redheaded matchmaker who fascinated him way too much for his own good.

Desperate measures were definitely needed. He looked at Phoebe and said, "Let's do it."

"You sure?" she asked with a level stare.

A man had to do what a man had to do. "I'm sure," he said. Because if agreeing to go out with Phoebe on a date put distance between him and Molly, and got her to leave him alone about dating, then that's what was necessary.

No matter what Molly's reaction might be.

Chapter Eight

Molly hurried back to the boutique with coffee and pastries in her hands, dodging raindrops as she went. Figured it would start raining just when she was caught outside without an umbrella. That was the Washington coast for you.

Luckily, she only had to go two blocks to get back to the warmth and dryness of her store; any farther and she would have been soaked.

Head down, she burst through the store's door and was attacked by a trio of excited dogs. After she hurriedly greeted them, then shooed them away, she looked up and was surprised to see Phoebe standing there, chatting with Grant.

Shaking off rain, Molly said, "Hey, Phoebs, what're you doing here so early?"

Phoebe was a notorious non-morning person and was rarely out of bed by 10:00 a.m. Fortunately, she had a wonderful employee who managed the ice cream store and always came in to open up in the morning.

"Oh, I…uh, had some errands to run, so I decided to stop by." She gave Grant a big smile that, to Molly, looked completely fake. "Grant and I have had a really, really nice conversation, haven't we?"

Molly looked questioningly at Grant, who seemed to be fascinated with something on the floor at the moment.

Without looking directly at Molly, he nodded and said, "Yup."

Disquieted by his odd manner, Molly turned her attention back to Phoebe; her friend was still smiling brightly. Too brightly. "Really?" Molly took off her coat, shook it out and then hung it up on the hook by the counter. "About what?"

Phoebe leaned on the counter. "You know how you've been trying to fix Grant and me up?"

"Yes," Molly replied, narrowing her eyes.

"Well, we've been talking, and…well, we'd like to go out on a date, after all."

Shockwaves rolled through Molly. She couldn't have been more surprised if Phoebe had announced she was moving to the North Pole to become one of Santa's elves. "You…have?"

"Yup," Phoebe said, nodding. She turned her

attention to Grant. "How does tonight work for you?"

He shook his head. "Tonight's a no-go. I have to get some work done."

"How about tomorrow night, then?" Phoebe asked.

In a flat voice, Grant said, "Fine."

Molly opened her mouth to speak, paused, then snagged a glance at Grant, who was staring intently at the floor again.

She frowned, then turned her attention back to Phoebe. "Why the sudden change of heart?"

"What do you mean?" Phoebe asked, her voice coated in pure innocence.

"Oh, come on, Phoebs," Molly said. "You're even more anti-dating than I am, which you confirmed when we talked last night. What's changed?"

Phoebe pushed off the counter. "I don't know." She shrugged. "I just think Grant's nice, and, really, what's the harm in having a bit of a social life?"

Molly didn't have a good answer for that because, technically, Phoebe was right.

A knot started to form in Molly's tummy. "Nothing, I guess. It just seems strange to me that you've suddenly decided to start dating, that's all."

"Isn't that what you wanted me to do?" Phoebe asked with a quirked brow. "You've been trying to shove me and Grant together since he arrived in town."

Very true. So why did she very much wish she hadn't?

Confusion spread through Molly. What was wrong with her, anyway? She wasn't usually so wishy-washy.

She cleared her throat. "Um…well, yes," she replied, trying to ignore the lump of dismay forming in her throat. "Of course."

"Then this is a good thing, right?" Phoebe said, spreading her arms wide. "Your current matchmaker goals will be all taken care of, your promise to Rose fulfilled and you can relax and simply enjoy Christmas."

Molly nodded, then went over to the front counter and looked for something casual to do. "Right, right," she replied, picking the stapler up and opening it to check to see if it had enough staples. Of course it did, so she slammed it closed, pinching her finger.

She cringed at the pain, shook her finger, then managed to say, "I think that's great you two have decided to go out." She put the stapler down and patted it. "Really, really great."

Grant pinned her in place with a pointed look. "You sure you don't mind?" he asked, his voice an odd monotone.

She did mind. A lot more than she should, or

than she'd expected. But that kind of thinking was silly. She didn't want to date Grant. There was no good reason Phoebe shouldn't. Right. Wonderful. Hooray.

This was what she'd wanted.

"Mind?" Molly said, turning toward him. "No, of course not." She smiled until it hurt. "Why would I mind?"

He put his hands in his jeans pockets and shrugged, his mouth a tight line. "I don't know...I just thought it might be a possibility."

He did? Why? "Nah, it's all good." She spied a slightly out of place can of dog food on an end-cap display and hurried over to straighten it. "I've thought all along you two would be perfect for each other, so, really, this is all working out the way it should."

"Oh, well, then," Grant said quickly. Emphatically. "Everybody's happy."

Molly's chest tightened and she stared at the cans of all-natural salmon-and-potato dog food for a second, gathering her control. She would not let this get to her. She. Would. Not. "Ecstatic," she said over her shoulder a moment later.

Then, before she could call the word back, she impulsively decided that the whole display needed to be redone. She quickly began unloading cans onto the floor, determined not to turn around and look at Grant to see if he was really as okay with going out with Phoebe as he seemed.

"So, Grant," Phoebe said. "Why don't we meet at Elly's Café tomorrow evening for meatloaf night."

"That sounds fine," he said. "What guy doesn't like meatloaf?"

"What time's good for you?" Phoebe asked. "I can get someone to cover for me at the shop, so anytime works for me."

Silence stretched out for a long moment.

To her absolute mortification, Molly's eyes burned. Suddenly, she stupidly wished that Grant would announce that he'd changed his mind and wanted to call the whole thing off.

But he didn't announce any such thing. Instead, he finally said in an even voice, "How about eight?"

"Eight would be great," Phoebe replied.

Molly blinked the unwanted, unaccounted-for tears away and closed her eyes briefly, completely disgusted by letting this Grant-dating-Phoebe thing get to her. Then she clamped down on her lip with her teeth and forced herself to stay silent, all the while managing to look as if she were doing nothing more than rearranging cans of dog food.

Actually, she was quite proud of herself.

Because deep down, where she'd trained herself not to look, unexpected pain had burrowed deep into her heart, and just the thought of Grant and Phoebe together made her feel as she had for most of her childhood—hollow and alone.

And without a clue as to how to handle the disconcerting, unwelcome emotions.

At precisely eight o'clock the next night, Grant walked into Elly's Café, which was located on Main Street just three doors down from Molly's store. The scent of meatloaf and potatoes hit him full force, and his heart twisted; his mom—a phenomenal cook—had made the best meatloaf he'd ever had.

Man, he missed her.

His eyes suddenly misty, he scanned the busy restaurant to distract himself from his grief. The place was exploding with Christmas decorations of every shape, size and variation of green, red, silver and gold in the Christmas rainbow.

A huge decorated Douglas Fir graced the far right corner, and a fire crackled away in the large rock fireplace that took up most of the other wall. Stockings hung from the rough-hewn wooden mantel, and a giant evergreen wreath bedecked with pinecones and a red-and-green-plaid ribbon hung over the entire thing.

After a second look around, he determined that Phoebe hadn't arrived yet. Just as he was about to sit down in the waiting area, an older woman with short blond hair who looked to be the hostess approached him.

"You must be Grant," she said with a friendly smile.

He pulled in his chin. "How did you know?"

"I'm Marie Graham. My son Seth is married to your cousin, Kim. We're practically relatives."

"Aha. I've been looking forward to meeting you." He stuck out his hand. "Aunt Rose told me all about you."

"And me, you," Marie replied, shaking his hand. "How's it going with Jade?"

He made a so-so motion with his hand. "She needs a lot of attention, and I'm working, so starting tomorrow Molly Kent is watching her during the day for me."

Marie beamed. "I heard."

"You did?" he asked, scratching his chin.

She leaned in. "I also know you're meeting Phoebe Sellers here for dinner."

Guess that was a small town for you. He wasn't sure he liked everyone knowing his business. "Yes, I am," he said, glancing around. "I don't think she's here yet."

"She's not, but I'll be happy to seat you." Marie winked. "I've reserved a special table for you two."

He swallowed. Hard. This whole thing was getting way out of hand. But it wasn't Marie's fault he'd agreed to this harebrained plan of Phoebe's. He alone bore the responsibility for this ill-advised "date."

"Great," he said in a strangled voice. "Lead the way."

Marie grabbed some menus from a small desk in the reception area, then headed across the restaurant.

Grant followed her to a two-person table in a cozy nook adjacent to the fireplace.

He sat, feeling like a fraud. This table should be reserved for happy, genuine couples, not two people trying to get a matchmaker to back off.

Marie handed him a menu with a flourish. "Here's the menu, but everybody comes on Thursdays for the meatloaf."

"I've heard."

"I'll send Phoebe over when she arrives," Marie said. "Can I get you anything to drink?"

"I could use some water, please." Suddenly, his throat felt dry. And…had his neck grown? His shirt collar suddenly felt way too tight.

"Water, coming right up," Marie said, leaving the table.

Once he was alone, he sat back and tried to relax and simply enjoy some downtime, but that proved difficult. This plan of Phoebe's just wasn't sitting well with him at all. It hadn't from the start.

Maybe that was because of Molly's shell-shocked expression when Phoebe had told her they wanted to go out. The hurt, surprised look on Molly's face had been like a sharp kick in his gut.

He pulled on his collar. Guess he'd just have to have dinner with Phoebe and then go on his merry way and head home to get back to work. He snagged a glance at his watch. He could be out of here by nine-fifteen, tops, no worse for the wear. And thanks to the work he'd done today, maybe he'd actually get some sleep tonight.

Luckily he'd managed to find Molly's tax files and have everything in order for her appointment with the IRS scheduled for yesterday afternoon. If he'd failed her there, he would have even more on his mind at the moment.

Marie brought two waters and set them on the table with a wink. He chugged his down fast. Better. But his collar still felt like a noose.

A few minutes later, he looked up, floored to see Molly headed toward his table, bundled up in an emerald green coat. His heart did a funny two-step. She seemed to get prettier every time he saw her. Only now, she appeared to be scowling. Though on her, even a scowl looked amazing.

He stood when she arrived at his table. "Hey, Molly," he said, unable to help smiling broadly. "What's up?" A thought occurred to him. "Did everything go all right with the guy from the IRS yesterday?" He'd found the files she'd needed buried deep in an incorrect folder.

"What? Oh, yeah. I had everything I needed, thanks to you."

"So what's wrong?"

She sighed and rolled her eyes. "Phoebe just called. The person who was supposed to cover for her at work didn't show."

Relief loosened his collar. "So she isn't coming," he stated.

"I'm afraid not." Molly pursed her lips. "I'm sorry she stood you up."

He wasn't. Not at all. "No problem. I understand." Maybe that was because he felt as if he'd been let off a very sharp hook he hadn't meant to get stuck on.

Molly paused, opened her mouth, then clamped it closed quickly. She lifted her chin. "So…er, anyway, now that I've delivered that message— in person, as Phoebe demanded—I'll be going."

His ears perked up. "Phoebe insisted you come here to tell me?"

Molly sighed and roughly hiked her purse onto her shoulder. "Yes. She was actually a little pushy, even for Phoebe."

Grant opened his mouth to reply, then noticed Marie standing nearby, smiling, eagerly looking back and forth between him and Molly.

Understanding dawned. No wonder Phoebe had been so insistent that they go out; she'd had an ulterior motive all along—to get him and Molly together. And Marie was in on the whole thing. Hence the "special" table.

He chastised himself; he was an idiot and should have seen Phoebe's scheme coming from a mile away. Sleep deprivation must have dulled his instincts. He was usually sharper than this.

He suddenly wished he'd been on his game a bit more so he could have nixed Phoebe's not-so-brilliant idea from the get-go. Now he had no choice but to let Molly in on what he and Phoebe had cooked up.

He cleared his throat, prepared to spill and face the consequences, even though the thought of losing Molly's presence in his life bothered him more than it should. "Um…Molly, I think we've been had."

She grimaced. "What do you mean?"

He walked over and pulled out the chair on the other side of the small table. "Why don't you have a seat and I'll tell you."

Her emerald eyes wide, she silently obliged.

Grant went back to his chair and sat, uneasiness chomping through him, setting his nerves on an uncomfortable edge. He could only hope that Molly would forgive him for being less than straight with her.

But, really, she had every right to withhold forgiveness and walk away.

And, astonishingly, that sobering truth felt like a blow to the very core of his heart.

Chapter Nine

"Why don't you take your coat off," Grant said to Molly, his mouth compressed in a fine line. "The fire is pretty warm."

A wave of worry swept through Molly as she set her purse down and then unbuttoned her coat and draped it over the back of her chair.

"What's going on?" She clenched her hands in a knot in her lap. "How have we been *had*?"

Grant placed his forearms on the table, leaning in. "Remember how you said that you were surprised Phoebe wanted to go out with me because she was even more anti-dating than you?"

Molly nodded slowly, bewildered. "I remember."

"Well, the truth is, Phoebe is still anti-dating."

"I don't understand," Molly replied. "If she still doesn't want to date, why did she suggest this dinner with you?"

Grant hesitated, his eyes reflecting what Molly would swear was pained regret. "So you'd back off trying to set us up."

She twitched her chin, blinking. "So she didn't really want to go out with you?"

"Nope. We just really wanted to prove to you that we weren't a good match."

Startling relief had Molly loosening her tightly gripped hands; Phoebe wasn't interested in Grant after, all! She wasn't sure why that was such good news, though....

All of a sudden, however, Phoebe's odd behavior made some sense. Even so, Molly was a bit shocked by her friend's cunning.

"That little schemer," Molly said with a quick shake of her head. "I'm going to have to have a talk with her."

Talk with Phoebe... Molly remembered the conversation she and Phoebe had had a few days ago when Phoebe had told Molly that she thought Molly should be the one to go out with Grant.

Suddenly, the real truth of the current situation dawned on Molly. Phoebe's stunt had been two-pronged: one, to get Molly to back off about setting Phoebe up with Grant, and two, to shove Molly and Grant together tonight!

Very clever, indeed.

"She was also trying to get you and me together, wasn't she?" Molly's cheeks warmed. "As I told you, she thinks I should be dating."

Grant nodded, his jaw visibly tight. "I think so," he said. "That's why I said we'd been *had*. She tricked me, too."

"Well, she was successful getting us together," Molly replied rucfully. "Here I am."

Grant cleared his throat and pulled on his collar. "I'm ashamed to admit that I agreed to the whole thing, so Phoebe wasn't the only one scheming." His eyes filled with a decidedly remorseful light. "I was a willing accomplice to the part where she was trying to get you to back off, and for that, I'm sorry."

Belatedly, Molly realized the truth in his statement; he'd gone along with the whole thing. But obviously he'd been in the dark about the other prong of Phoebe's plan. Oddly, she wished his motives had been reversed.

Good grief. She was losing her marbles for sure.

She gave herself a mental shake to clear her thoughts and regain her hold on her sanity. "Why didn't you just tell me you didn't want to go out with Phoebe?"

His stormy blue gaze collided with hers. "I did. Several times."

Face-heating shame marched through her. She shouldn't have pushed so hard to get them together. "And I didn't listen, did I?"

He shook his head. "Phoebe and I felt trapped, and we thought this was the only way to get you to stop."

She cringed, ashamed she'd pushed them to this. "Sorry. I guess I went a little overboard with the matchmaking stuff." She'd been so eager to get Grant off the market, she hadn't heeded his and Phoebe's wishes, not that she'd share the getting-him-off-the-market part with Grant.

"Can I ask you a favor?" he said, interrupting the disconcerting path of her thoughts.

"Sure."

"Can you please stop trying to set me up on dates?" He shook his head. "I know it's your thing and all, but as I've said before, I'm really not interested in dating anyone and it's time for it to end."

She looked at her hands in her lap. She hadn't listened to him in the first place. And look how it had backfired on her.

She needed to back off.

Clearing her throat, she said, "Of course. I'm sorry I didn't get the message sooner."

"No problem, as long as we're on the same page now."

"We are," she said. "Not that there aren't a lot of women who would be all over going out with you—"

"Molly," he warned, giving her a stern look.

"Just sayin'…" She grinned to let him know she was joking.

He returned her smile, flashing his straight white teeth. "Yeah, yeah. I know. But with you it's always more than just talk."

"Yeah, it's a problem," she said, telling herself she'd been just as much a schemer as Phoebe. Molly had had her own ulterior motive for trying to fix Phoebe and Grant up, one she wasn't particularly proud of at the moment.

"Well, I was part of the problem," Grant said. "Can you forgive me?" he asked, hitting her with those blue eyes of his.

Molly's heart softened. Who could refuse a sincere apology like that from a stand-up man like Grant? Forgiveness was definitely the right thing to do, especially given that she was just as guilty as they were.

"Of course I can forgive you," she said. "No hard feelings at all."

"Great." He gave an exaggerated wipe to his brow, as if to say "whew." "I was worried you'd never talk to me again."

She blinked. He'd been worried? About never talking to her again? Why did that make her feel just a little bit happy? All right, a *lot* happy?

She hastily took a sip of water. The answer was too scary, too significant, to even contemplate right now. She'd figure it out later. Maybe.

When she could handle the truth. *If* she could handle the truth....

"Nah," she said in a nonchalant way she didn't really feel. "You're a nice guy. No reason to hold one little mistake against you."

"Well, I appreciate you going easy on me." He pinned her with a pointed stare. "You going to go as easy on Phoebe?"

Molly paused. She'd have to; Phoebe hadn't been any more manipulative than Molly herself had been. "Yes, I am," she said. "We've been friends too long to hold this little stunt against her."

"I'm glad to hear that," Grant replied, leaning forward. "She only had your best interests at heart."

"I know." Molly gave him a small smile. "I'm not used to being the matchmakee, though." She preferred to be in charge of her own destiny, with God's guidance. While she believed in her own matchmaking instincts—obviously—she was adamant about remaining on the setting-up end of things rather than the other way around.

"I'm not, either," Grant replied with a rueful grin that made his eyes sparkle appealingly. "So let's not look at this as an official date. Let's just look at it as two friends enjoying the best meat-loaf on the coast together."

Her tummy dipped. "You're asking me to stay?"

she said, speaking evenly despite the anticipation bouncing around in her like a kid on her way to Disneyland.

"It's the least I can do after conspiring against you with Phoebe."

"Well, in that case, I accept your invitation," Molly said, unwilling to examine too closely why she was looking so forward to spending time with Grant.

The terrifying truth sure wasn't going anywhere, and would be there when she had no choice but to examine it.

With her stomach tied in little but unsettling knots, Molly was surprised she'd managed to eat a thing sitting across the table from Grant.

But Elly's meatloaf was Elly's meatloaf, and Molly had put away her serving pretty well considering she was having dinner with the most attractive man she'd run across in a long, long time.

A man she was supposed to be keeping her distance from. But wasn't. Not even a little bit at the moment.

Oh, well. The past forty-five minutes spent with Grant were now officially in the water-under-the-bridge category—she couldn't turn back time, change things and leave him sitting here alone.

So she'd enjoy the rest of her meal—which shouldn't be hard considering the charming company and the dessert she was planning on having—then reinforce the lock on her heart and throw the key in the Pacific Ocean a block away.

Relaxing a bit, Molly read the dessert menu in her hand, her mouth watering. She had a sweet tooth that wouldn't leave her alone for anything. "What sounds good to you?"

Grant looked at her over the paper menu he held. "I'm stuffed, but I'm a sucker for tiramisu."

She put her hand on her tummy. "I'm full, too, but could probably be convinced to shovel in some dessert." She had to at least *act* like she ate healthily.

"Should we share?" he asked, one brow lifted slightly.

She blinked. "Sure," she said, absolutely not wanting to make a big deal out of the implied intimacy of sharing a dessert. If Grant didn't think eating a decadent treat off the same plate was a problem, then neither did she.

"I love Tiramisu." And she just didn't have it in her to turn down an opportunity to indulge in her favorite dessert. Call her weak and dessert-challenged.

Marie came over and took their dessert order, her eyes twinkling when Grant told her to bring one dessert and two spoons. Fortunately, she didn't comment on their idea to share; as long as no one else made a big deal out of the "datelike" situation that really wasn't a date at all, but felt like one, Molly wouldn't, either.

Not a *big* deal, anyway.

Grant sat back, his chiseled chin tilted at an angle, a light smile playing about his lips. He looked so handsome sitting there in his dark gray pants, paired with a medium blue sweater that emphasized his broad shoulders and made his impossibly blue eyes even bluer, his short blond hair attractively disheveled. Clean-cut had always appealed to her…but Grant…well, he gave new meaning to the words.

She mentally scoffed. Computer nerd, her foot. The man was downright gorgeous. And charming. Unluckily for her.

And with him smiling at her like that, looking so good she could barely breathe, she again found herself wishing she wasn't so drawn to handsome, appealing, little old him.

She took a sip of water, breathed again, then gave voice to a tangent of her distressing thoughts. "So were you really a nerd growing up?"

"Still having trouble with that one?"

"Honestly, yes." She made a face. "You just aren't very…nerdlike."

"Well, I've had a lot of time to figure out how not to *look* like a nerd."

Yeah. She'd noticed. More than a few times.

"But back then." He grimaced. "Whoa. It was bad."

She shook her head. "Every kid goes through that awkward phase."

"No, see, I was beyond awkward. I had bad skin, ugly glasses, no sense of style, and grew so much my freshman year in high school, I was a major string bean for about two years."

"I can't picture you like that." Maybe if she could, she'd be able to put him out of her mind. Of course, he was a really good guy, too, which rounded out the package quite well, and made it that much more difficult to ignore him. She'd have to try harder.

"Believe it. I was a bookworm, too, and studied a lot, so I had zero social life," he said.

Too bad none of those high school girls had looked beyond Grant's geeky outer package to see the wonderful person hiding underneath. "I bet you were the straight-A student who ruined the bell curve for the rest of us, weren't you?" she said with a teasing grin.

He tilted his head to the side and nodded in acknowledgment. "Yup, that was me. I used to pride myself on getting the highest grade in the class. I actually went a whole year with nothing but 100 percent on every one of my tests."

"So high school was easy for you," she stated.

"Academically, yes. But socially?" He shook his head. "No way."

Marie graciously interrupted to set their tiramisu on the table between them. "Here you go." She handed them each a spoon. "Enjoy sharing, you two!" she said, her eyes glowing with undisguised delight, her mouth pulled up into an unmistakably pleased smile.

Molly smiled back, unable to help letting herself get a teensy bit caught up in Marie's happiness. Temporarily, at least. But she'd have to nip the feeling in the bud before long, or risk going to a place called heartbreak. "Thanks, Marie. It looks scrumptious."

After Marie left, Molly said, "So you weren't a social butterfly?"

"Absolutely not," he replied with an under-the-breath laugh, then gestured to the tiramisu with his spoon. "Ladies first."

She obliged, appreciating his manners, and took a big spoonful of dessert. The flavors of coffee, cream and rich lady fingers exploded in her mouth. "Oh, my goodness, that's good."

Grant took a spoonful, rolling his eyes as he chewed. "Delicious."

When he was done with that bite, he said, "I was different in high school, and I didn't fit in. Not exactly a recipe for having lots of friends."

"High school can be a cruel place for kids who

are different," she said, empathizing with him; she'd felt odd because she'd hadn't had a mother, and because her dad was so disconnected with her life and had never shown up for anything.

"I bet you fit in just fine," Grant replied after he took another bite of tiramisu. "You get along with everybody."

"I do all right now, but I had my awkward moments when I was growing up," she said. "Everybody does."

"Well, I had more than my share. I once asked a girl to the prom, and she actually laughed in my face while turning me down." He shook his head. "I was crushed."

Molly's heart broke for him. "Sounds like she didn't deserve a nice guy like you."

"Well, that's easy to see now, of course, but at the time, it was devastating." He put his spoon down. "I actually saw her at my ten-year high school reunion, and after we talked and she found out what I did for a living, she slipped me her phone number under the table." He shrugged. "Guess she had a change of heart."

Not surprising. A successful, friendly, good-looking guy like Grant probably had lots of women interested in him.

"What did you do?" she asked, more curious than she should be about how he handled a woman blatantly hitting on him. "Turn her down cold, like she did to you?"

"Believe me, I thought about it."

"Who wouldn't?" He was human, after all.

"Exactly. But being deliberately cruel isn't my style. I called her the next day and politely told her that I didn't date because I was too busy."

His unwillingness to be mean to someone who'd been cruel to him awed her to the core, affirming that he was a genuinely kind, compassionate person.

Panic chipped away at her. Desperately grasping at something—anything—to balance out how impressed she was with him, she said, "And that's the truth, your too-busy-to-date policy." She looked right at him, facing her fears head-on. "Isn't it?"

Grant gave her a funny look. "Yup, sure is," he said with a quick nod. "My job is the most important thing in my life."

No surprise there. He was just like her dad, meaning too busy with his job for anyone but himself. Was there a better way to remind herself that she had no business falling for Grant?

Nope. Sure wasn't.

Now she just needed to heed the warning.

Chapter Ten

Fifteen minutes after Grant and Molly finished dessert, they stepped out of Elly's Café into the cool, crisp, ocean-scented air and began walking down the Main Street boardwalk in the direction of her store.

A stiff breeze blew, like it almost always did around here, but the rain hadn't started again, and it was really a pretty nice night for December on the coast.

Grant slanted a glance at Molly as she buttoned up. He again noticed how pretty she looked in the green coat that complemented her fair skin and brought out the copper strands in her fiery wind-whipped hair, illuminated by the clear Christmas lights wrapped around every streetlamp next to the boardwalk.

He frowned when he saw that her fine-boned jaw seemed tight. In fact, she'd seemed to clam up right about the time they'd finished the tiramisu.

Maybe her closing off had been a good thing, actually. He wasn't used to opening up to people, letting them see the real him.

But still, what had caused her to shut down? Had he said or done something wrong?

He thought they'd had a very enjoyable dinner, in fact. Of course, he didn't get out much and hadn't been on an actual date since…who knew when. But even so, he'd really liked talking with Molly, listening to her laugh, the way her green eyes had darkened in the firelight. More than he probably should.

And now here they were, and their evening was over. He was surprised to realize part of him didn't want to say goodbye just yet. He felt at ease with Molly. Content. And…*happy*.

Red flags whipped in the whirlwind of his mind. He reminded himself what he'd told her— this evening wasn't a date, even if it had felt like one. It would be best to say goodbye now, before he forgot they weren't on a romantic dinner outing and did something he'd regret.

Like pulling her close and running his fingers through that gold-tinted mass of hair. Dipping his head for a tender kiss. Feeling the curve of her delicate jaw.

He sucked in a huge gulp of bracing air, striving for control. By force, he reminded himself that he hadn't come to Moonlight Cove for any kind of romance; he'd come to take care of his aunt's dog and work his fingers off to meet his deadline.

No matter how he looked at the situation, excelling at his job and letting himself get caught up in the beautiful, sweet, wonderful woman next to him just didn't go together. And never would. No matter what stories he told himself along the way.

That sobering thought prompted him to push out, "I really should head home." Tick-tock.

"Okay," she said, throwing him a shy, gentle smile that made his knees weak. She stopped walking as they reached the corner. "I'm going this way," she said, pointing to the street straight ahead, which led away from her store. "Thanks for dinner. I had a nice time."

"I did, too." He puckered his brow. "Aren't you going to get your car?"

She shoved her wind-tossed hair behind her ear. "No. I walked to work today, and Gena took Peter and Parker to my house after she closed the store."

His protective instincts surged, and he stepped forward. "You shouldn't be walking around at night alone."

"Moonlight Cove is pretty safe," she replied. "I'll be fine."

He wasn't about to find out whether she was right. "No way. I'd never forgive myself if something happened to you." He held out his arm.

"I walked here, too, so I'm walking you home, no arguments."

She paused, her chin up, then tilted her head to the side. "I...guess you're right," she said.

"Good. Because I'm not changing my mind."

Her eyes turned up to his. "Should we walk on the beach?"

With his free hand he gestured to the right. "Lead the way," he said, telling himself he'd agreed because he needed the exercise to work off the huge dinner he'd eaten.

"Maybe we'll get a peek at the moon," she said, her voice wistful. "I'll bet it's beautiful tonight."

He gave in to the gentle pressure of her arm and fell in step beside her.

Guess he'd worry about the inevitable consequences of strolling on the beach with Molly later.

Illuminated by the full moon peeking out from behind the clouds, the beach stretched out before Molly as she stepped onto the sand, grasping Grant's firm upper arm. He was a silent yet considerably profound presence there in the dark with the ocean waves crashing to shore just fifty or so feet ahead of them, and she couldn't manage to conjure up words, either.

Honestly, she was stunned he agreed to stay with her a bit longer, given his hardheaded insistence on making a computer mouse his only pet and the guy who announced he had emails his only friend.

But…she couldn't deny that she was thrilled, too, and touched by his wanting to keep her safe. Deep down, she was also scared silly to be letting herself extend their evening like this.

She chided herself. This was just a walk on the beach. No biggie. Or it shouldn't be, at least.

The tide was high, so the beach was narrow. Before long, they reached the hard sand next to the waterline and, in sync and without words, stopped to gaze at the moon casting its silver light down onto the ocean from overhead.

She stood there in silence for a few long moments, enjoying the sight, her hand still holding on to his warm arm. The wind kicked up, blowing her hair around, and a shiver ran through her.

"Are you cold?" he asked, turning to look at her.

She corralled her hair, then returned his gaze, noting that the light of the moon cast his face in shadows, highlighting his cheeks and nose, making him appear mysterious. Exceedingly striking. And dangerously inviting.

She swallowed, thrown off by the intimacy of being here with this incredibly attractive man. Another gust of wind blew the hem of her coat out, allowing chilly air in. She involuntarily wiggled her knees to ward off the cold breeze blowing in from the Pacific.

"A little bit."

"Here," he said, lifting his arm up and over her so that it lay across her shoulders. "I'll keep you warm." Then he gently pulled her close, into the perfectly sized curve of his lean body.

She stiffened, trying to remember her promise to herself to keep things impersonal. Strictly admiration from afar.

But then the warmth of his body sunk in, and all of her vows dissipated like rain on hot pavement. Another kind of shiver—the good kind— ran through her, breaking her will to resist him into a million pieces.

With an internal sigh of surrender, she snuggled into him, her cheek laying against the side of his chest, her arm going around his broad, well-muscled back. His other arm came up and wrapped around her from the front, settling her more fully into his embrace.

Despite the stiff breeze blowing, the subtle scent of his aftershave and soap, all spicy and fresh, hit her full force. He was warm and cozy and solid, and he smelled better than any man had a right to. Being here in his arms felt so perfect. Comforting. Safe.

"You were right," he said softly, squeezing her shoulder, his breath whispering across her hair. "The moon is beautiful tonight."

She nodded. "It's not called Moonlight Cove for nothing."

"I can see that," he replied with a chuckle.

A distant memory surfaced. "When I was little, whenever we came to Moonlight Cove, my mom brought me to the beach to hunt for the moon."

She felt him pull away slightly to look down at her. "That sounds like a good memory."

She looked out at the dark, roiling ocean, blinking. "Some of the only ones I have of my childhood."

"Really?" he asked, his voice tinged with what sounded like sympathy.

"Pretty much." She gave a humorless laugh. "After my mom died...well, my dad didn't have a lot of time for me." As in *none*.

"You want to talk about it?" Grant went silent as one hand began rubbing her shoulder soothingly, tenderly, waiting, it seemed, for her to finish. Or not. Somehow she had a feeling he wouldn't push her. Bless him for that.

The wind gusted again, and she pressed closer to Grant, needing his warmth. His support. His understanding.

Feeling something let loose inside, Molly continued on, needing to unburden herself. To give in to Grant's unspoken invitation to lean on him. Good or bad, she wanted to talk.

"We certainly never came back here to hunt for

the moon. He was so immersed in his work, we never went on another vacation." She shrugged, trying for a casualness she didn't feel to somehow minimize what she was about to say; the words and thoughts hurt less that way. For a while, at least.

Grant waited a beat to respond. "I'm so sorry," he said, his hand coming up to caress her cheek. "Sounds like your dad wasn't really there for you when you needed him."

A lump formed in her throat and her eyes burned. "No, he wasn't." She sniffed. "He still isn't, even though he's been calling lately, wanting to see me."

Grant turned so he was fully facing her, but kept his arms around her. "How do you feel about that?"

She let out a shaky sigh. "I've refused so far."

"Because?" Grant prompted, his hands rubbing her back in circles.

Her threatening tears welled and spilled over her eyelids. She just shook her head, too ashamed to admit that she didn't know how to forgive her own father. Did that make her a terrible person? Sometimes she felt like the most horrible daughter around.

"It's okay," Grant said, ever so gently wiping her tears away with his thumbs. "You can tell me. I'm not going to judge you."

She believed him. Though she'd known Grant only a short time, she could read people pretty well; she knew deep in her heart that he wasn't a judgmental or presumptuous person.

So she swallowed, and pulled back, needing space. Then she forced out, "Try as I might, pray as I might, I just don't know how to forgive him for emotionally abandoning me."

"It's hard to forgive those who've hurt us, isn't it?"

She could only nod.

For a few seconds all she could hear was the wind and the crashing waves.

Finally, Grant spoke. "Just a thought, but doesn't the Bible say we should forgive those who trespass against us?"

"Yes, it does," she replied, nodding in agreement. Everyone knew the Lord's Prayer. "But sometimes, even if we know what we should do— in my case, forgiving my dad—actually doing the right thing is difficult. Even if the Bible lays it out for you."

"I hear you there," he replied, a hint of ruefulness in his voice. "Loud and clear."

Tilting her chin, she gazed at him speculatively. "You sound like you speak from experience."

His face froze, and he seemed to fold inward. He dropped his arm and closed his eyes briefly, only to open them to stare out at the ocean glimmering ever so slightly in the reflection of the moon's glow.

Suddenly, she felt cold. And alone. And it had a lot more to do with the loss of his warmth than the fact that it was a chilly night on the beach in December. She studied him, standing just two feet from her, his shoulders hunched, his hands now in his pockets. He looked as if he felt chilled to the bone, too.

She lifted her chin. No reason they should both feel that way, though she understood his need to put up walls. Talking about your pain was, well, painful. Difficult. Yet brave and cleansing, too.

He needed to open up as much as she did.

Shaking with more than just cold, she reached out and touched him. "You can talk to me." She rubbed his forearm. "I won't judge you, either, you know."

His gaze flew to hers. "I didn't think you would."

"Then why are you pulling away?"

He shifted uneasily, but she kept her hand on him. "It's hard to talk about my mom."

She'd had a niggling feeling this was about his mother. "I know. But I think you'll probably feel better if you do."

He regarded her, deep emotional pain emanating from his eyes. Then he nodded as he reached out and grabbed her hand and held it tight.

"It's okay," she said, gripping his hand.

After a long pause, he said, "The truth is...I can't forgive God for taking my mom from me."

Her heart clenched. "So you *do* know what I'm talking about," she stated.

All she got from him was a nod.

"Have you taken your own advice and looked to the Bible for help?"

"As you said, doing the right thing isn't always easy."

"What about prayer?" she asked, pulling him along toward her house. The cold and wind were beginning to get to her now that Grant wasn't warming her up from the inside out. "I often find praying helpful when I don't know what to do or how to do it."

He started walking beside her, still holding her hand. "I haven't even been able to do that."

"Why not?"

"I prayed to God and asked Him to heal her, and He left my prayers unanswered."

She knew where this was going. "So I take it you've lost faith?" she asked, a lump forming in her heart.

"Pretty much. Why pray if God isn't listening?"

"Just because you didn't get the answer you wanted doesn't mean He's not listening."

Grant shot her an exasperated look.

She squeezed his hand. "God says yes, no or

not now, just like the rest of us. So He did listen," she explained softly. "Right?"

Grant looked at the dark night sky, his jaw flexing before he spoke. "But I wanted her to be healed...."

"And she has been—in heaven."

"I know that here," he said, pointing to his head. "But here?" He put a hand over his heart. "Here I miss her so much it hurts. And my dad...well, he just hasn't been the same, and I doubt he'll ever be."

"He still has you, right?" she said.

Grant nodded. "Yes, he does. But I'm not sure I'm enough."

"I know that feeling," she said, resuming their walk, his large, warm hand still enveloping hers in a very comforting way.

"How so?"

Call her crazy, but opening up just seemed like the right thing to do. "Ever since my father abandoned me, I've always felt like I'll never be enough."

Grant stopped dead, pulling on her hand to bring her to a halt. "Whoa, whoa, wait a minute."

She halted and swung her gaze to him.

His jaw had visibly dropped. "You're everything to everyone, one of the most giving people I've ever met. How can you possibly feel you're not enough?"

His words were a soothing balm to some portions of her heart, but she knew a good part remained wounded and scarred and, she feared, always would.

"My own father left me alone through my whole childhood," she said, her voice cracking despite her best efforts to stay in control. "I wasn't enough for him to love me just a little bit...."

Instantly, Grant pulled her into his arms. "Don't ever talk that way," he said next to her ear, his slightly stubbly jaw rough against her cheek. "You're a wonderful person through and through. Don't ever doubt that."

His words of praise chipped away at the guardrails on her heart, opening up a floodgate of emotion she was helpless to hold in. "How can I not? Every person I've ever loved has left me."

Pulling back, he slid his hands up and under her hair to cup both sides of her jaw. He looked right at her, his face just inches from hers, his blue eyes shining with absolute conviction. "Well, they were fools to walk away from someone as amazing as you."

His words thawed yet another corner of her heart, creating a healing, warm completion she'd never felt before. Never even imagined. Why was she working so hard to keep him away? Right now, she couldn't begin to remember, much less fight his pull.

"Really?"

"Really," he said, before he closed the distance between them and gently, tenderly kissed her.

Molly sucked in a shocked breath as his lips claimed hers, then slid her arms around his waist and kissed him back, reveling in the solidness of his broad chest against her. Instantly, a feeling of safety and contentment settled around her, and she wanted to draw on his warmth and strength forever.

But a tiny echo in her brain told her that nothing lasted forever. Especially not love.

Unable to ignore the whisper of caution, she ended the kiss and stepped back, out of Grant's embrace. She stared at him, her breathing fast, her whole body yearning to be back in his arms.

But that would be a mistake, with a price she wasn't willing to pay.

He stared intently back. "Molly..."

Holding up a hand, she said, "That was a slip-up."

"Did it really feel like a mistake to you?" he asked, his voice low and rough. Disbelieving?

No. Kissing him had felt so right. Perfect in so many ways. But none of that mattered. What felt *right* wasn't always the same as what was actually *safe;* she'd learned that lesson the painful way, several times.

"I can't let myself get carried away by emotion."

She put her clenched hands in her coat pockets. "Can you?"

She waited for him to answer, hoping in some foolish, naive part of her mind that he would refute her statement and pull her back into the safe, warm haven of his arms. And never let her go.

Just the thought made her knees weak.

Instead, he looked at her for a long moment, jerked a hand through his wind-mussed hair, then dropped his gaze to the sand. "No, I guess I can't."

Expected. She drew herself up despite her noodly legs, and said in an amazingly brisk tone, "Good, then we're on the same page." The only possible end to their story.

So why did she want to press herself back into his arms and stay there forever?

Grant walked home after he said goodbye to Molly on her doorstep, his thoughts chaotic. It had started to rain just about the time they'd arrived at her house, and the wind had picked up, too. A storm outside to match the storm inside of him. Figured, didn't it?

He couldn't stop thinking about what she'd said about God listening to his prayers.

One the surface her wise words had made sense. But underneath, in his heart of hearts, a part of him wanted to denounce what Molly had said; her opinions challenged him in a way that made him uncomfortable, a way that would force him to face his problems with God.

And deal with his grief. The thought was too difficult to handle.

Then there was their kiss. Wow. Just…wow. He was twenty-eight years old and in all those years… Molly was…so Molly. But thank goodness she'd had the sense to break off the kiss because, well, he sure wouldn't have.

He scrubbed a hand over his face as he rounded the corner to Aunt Rose's street. Molly had fried a couple of his circuits. He needed a boatload of surge protectors to keep from overheating around her.

Not what he wanted. He needed his circuits now more than ever. He needed to be pushing Molly away, not pulling her closer.

He couldn't afford to forget that a second time.

Chapter Eleven

The day after he and Molly kissed on the beach, Grant sat at his computer, staring blankly at the screen, willing his brain to focus on work rather than thoughts of Molly.

With a grunt of frustration, he shot to his feet and rubbed his burning eyes. He just couldn't concentrate on his work, and he was getting nowhere in the production department, fast. And Jade wasn't even around; he'd dropped her off at Molly's store this morning.

If he kept on this don't-work-and-hang-out-with-Molly path, he'd never make his deadline.

Try as he might, though, he just couldn't get her out of his mind. Their conversation on the beach ran around and around in his brain, an endless loop filled with a glut of questions, thoughts, detailed analyses and vivid memories that were slowly driving him to utter distraction.

And their kiss? Unforgettable.

His hands on his hips, he sightlessly stared out at the ocean, shaking his head. Molly challenged him in so many ways, and he wasn't sure how to deal with that.

But he'd need to figure out that problem, and soon. Or he wouldn't have a job.

Talk about high stakes.

Just as he was sitting down to get back to the never-ending battle with his code, a knock on the front door sounded. He frowned, then rose. He wasn't expecting anyone....

Rubbing his stiff neck, he headed over and opened the door.

Pleasure amped through him at the sight of Molly in her green coat, a white knit scarf and matching hat perched jauntily on top of her red curls. Out of nowhere, he had the sudden urge to bend down and kiss her hello.

Back up, Roderick.

She waved with the hand not holding Jade's leash, a cute little smile curving her glossy pink lips. "Hey. You ready?"

Blankly, he stared at her. "For what?"

"You and I are supposed to take Jade for her visit to the hospital children's ward today, remember?" She gave him a chiding look. "She goes every Friday."

He sighed, doing a mental forehead slap. The

activity had been noted on the calendar Aunt Rose had left, but in the craziness of being behind— and being so frustratingly hung up on Molly— he'd forgotten.

"I guess it slipped my mind," he replied. "Sorry, I've been really busy." And distracted. He was lucky if he managed to eat, much less remember appointments he wasn't used to keeping.

"Well, get ready quick," she said with a shooing motion. "We can still be on time if you hurry."

He stepped back, wondering helplessly how he was going to get out of going. The amount of time to his deadline was shrinking at an alarming rate. He'd made some progress on his project. But enough?

Molly followed him right in, Jade at her heels.

Taking a deep breath, he prepared to tell her he couldn't go.

Before he could, Molly piped in with, "Wait until you meet Katie."

"Katie?" he said as he pushed the door closed.

Molly's eyes brightened so much they resembled sunlit emeralds. "She's this one little girl who adores Jade."

"You know the kids?" He hadn't realized Molly was a regular part of Jade's therapy dog program.

"Of course. I try to go with Rose as often as I can," she replied, taking off her gloves. "I'm so fortunate, and the kids are so sick, it seems like the right thing to do, no matter how busy I am."

Guilt dug into him. "Why's Katie in the hospital?"

Molly's face grew serious. "She was in a very serious car accident, with lots of internal injuries and broken bones. She wasn't expected to live... so, it really lifts me up to be able to make her happy after all she's been through."

His chest tightened. Of course, it made sense a caring person like Molly would accompany Jade and Rose; Molly, along with his aunt, was one of the most giving, unselfish, compassionate people he'd ever met.

Shame danced with very sharp heels all around inside of him. Molly and his aunt made time for sick kids every Friday, week in and week out. His conscience tapped his shoulder, hard; how could he deliberately refuse to go today without looking—and worse yet, *feeling*—like a heartless jerk?

Frankly, he couldn't. Molly had shown him that life wasn't always about him.

His refusal died a quick, efficient death. "Let me get my coat."

"Okay, but step on it," Molly replied, grinning, her eyes sparkling in eager anticipation. "Some of the kids get tired the later it gets, and I want to be able to see all of them so no one is disappointed."

"I'll run," he said, deeply admiring her commitment to bringing happy moments into the lives of sick kids.

He hurried to the closet, reiterating to himself that being unselfish would ultimately bring good things into his life.

Even if being necessarily selfless was going to put a major kink in meeting his deadline.

Guess he'd just have to work all that much harder tomorrow. Too bad he wasn't sure that was remotely possible.

On the car ride to the hospital, most of Grant's tension had faded away as he'd listened to Molly animatedly talk about the kids they'd be visiting.

Now, as he walked across the parking lot with her, he slanted a chagrined glance at a wild and woolly Jade as she pranced merrily along beside them on her leash, her ears blowing in the stiff breeze. At one point she jumped in the air and spun halfway around before she landed on all fours.

"You really think she's going to calm down enough to visit sick kids?" he asked, skeptical.

"Don't worry," Molly replied with an easy smile. "Like most standard poodles, she's very smart and extremely intuitive. She knows when to calm down."

He had his doubts; she'd been pretty naughty in the past, and right now it looked as if she was getting ready to chase a fake bunny around a doggy racetrack as a warm-up for some canine gymnastics on the sidelines. "Whatever you say."

They entered the hospital and made their way past a large decorated Christmas tree to the third floor children's ward. Several employees waved and greeted Molly by name. Guess she really was a regular around here.

As soon as they entered the elevator, Jade sat obediently at Molly's heels without being asked, her ears forward, tail wagging against the floor ever so slightly.

When they got off the elevator and headed down a corridor on the right, all of Jade's wildness had been replaced by an amazing composure that really took Grant by surprise. Seemed the crazy mutt had an alter ego that knew how to behave. Where had that dog been when Mr. Hyde-like Jade had been driving him nuts?

As they approached the central nurses' station, which was decorated with poinsettias and shiny Christmas ornaments on ribbons hanging from the ceiling, a tall, older brunette woman dressed in blue scrubs rose from behind the desk and walked out to greet them. "Well, look who's here. Miss Jade and her helper."

"Hi, Patricia," Molly said as they moved closer. She gestured to Grant. "This is Grant Roderick,

Rose's nephew. Grant, this is Nurse Patricia, the day charge nurse."

Patricia smiled, then bent down to pet Jade, who'd obediently sat when they'd arrived at the desk. "You here to help Molly out?" Patricia asked Grant, looking up at him as she rubbed Jade's ears.

"Wouldn't miss it," he said truthfully.

"Great. We always like to see new faces." She straightened and turned her attention to Molly. "Katie's been asking for Jade," she said. "The nurse on the graveyard shift said Katie woke up very early this morning because she was so excited it was Jade's visiting day. Katie requested you stop there first. Would you mind?"

"Of course not," Molly said. "I'm looking forward to seeing Katie, too." She craned her neck to look down the hall. "Is she still in 308?"

"She sure is," Patricia replied, heading back behind the desk. "Go on down if you like."

Molly regarded him. "You ready?"

"Let's do it." Surprisingly, he was looking forward to seeing the kids, Katie in particular.

They went down the hallway and took a right into Katie's room. Grant followed Molly in, steeling himself to handle seeing an injured little girl.

Katie, a tiny blue-eyed blonde, lay propped up in the hospital bed with tubes and IVs hooked up to her. She was dressed in pink fleece pajamas with purple dogs all over them and fuzzy purple socks pulled over her toes. Her curly hair was braided into pigtails that trailed down over her narrow shoulders. Hot-pink casts covered both legs and one arm, and Grant noticed visible bruising on her face. An older nurse with short gray hair stood by her bed, adjusting her IV.

"Jadey's here!" Katie crowed, a smile as big as the sun on her face, having eyes only for Jade. "I've been waiting all day for you guys!"

"Hey there, Katie," Molly said cheerily as she led a remarkably composed Jade over to the side of the bed. "We stopped here first at your request, honey."

Katie held out her good arm, gesturing to Jade, who'd come to a stop next to the bed. "Help her up here. I want to hug her."

The older nurse said, "Hi, Molly. Katie's been waiting all morning for that darling dog."

Looked like Molly was on a first-name basis with almost everyone here.

"Hi, June. I heard." Turning to Katie, Molly said, "I gave her a bath this morning." Molly patted the foot of the bed. "She's all ready to snuggle."

"She looks like a little lamb," Katie said, gazing at Jade with something akin to wonder glinting from her eyes. "But she's a doggy!"

Remembering the havoc that *little lamb* had caused, Grant's gut clenched and he almost reached out a staying hand. But Jade gingerly jumped onto the bed where Molly had indicated, then slowly and carefully walked up and laid down next to Katie on the far side of the bed, putting her head ever so softly on Katie's chest.

Grant blinked. Was this the same dog that'd had him kissing pavement every time he tried to take her on a walk?

Katie instantly laid her uninjured arm over Jade, then pressed her cheek into the long, puffy hair on top of Jade's head and closed her eyes, her face relaxing into an expression of pure contentment. "Oh, Jadey-girl. I love you."

Grant's chest tightened at the look of happiness on Katie's face.

Nurse June waved and left the room.

Molly sat on the edge of the bed next to Katie, presumably to supervise, and Grant watched in wonder as Jade held perfectly still and let Katie hug her, pat her and press gentle kisses to her head. Who would have guessed that the dog who had driven him crazy with her naughty antics would behave so wonderfully, so gently now?

Certainly not him.

After a few moments of bestowing love on Jade, Katie lifted her casted arm and pointed at Grant. "Who's he?"

Molly stood and gently pulled on his arm. "This is my friend Grant Roderick. He's Miss Rose's nephew, and he's taking care of Jade while she's on vacation."

He waved. "Hi, Katie."

"Hi, Mr. Roderick," she replied, peering at him intently, appearing to size him up, her chin raised, her hands buried in Jade's woolly coat. "Is Jadey being a good girl for you?"

Being called Mr. Roderick made him feel like he was ancient, so he said, "You can call me Grant. And...um...well, yes, she is being pretty good." Right now she was, anyway, so he spoke the truth. "She looks like she's fond of you, so she's being extra good, isn't she?"

Katie pressed her face into Jade's head fur. "She's always extra good," Katie said, her words muffled by fur. "Aren't you, girl?"

Jade's tail quivered.

"She answered me!" Katie exclaimed, her blue eyes sparkling.

Grant's breath caught.

Molly stood and pulled an item out of her purse. "Do you want to help me brush Jade?" She held up a dog brush. "I brought her favorite."

Katie nodded, her eyes bright. "Okay! I love doing that."

"I know you do," Molly said as she sat next to

Katie and Jade on the bed. "That's why I brought this, silly." She handed the brush to Katie.

Grant couldn't take his eyes off Molly.

Beaming, Katie took the brush in her good hand and gently began running it through Jade's ear fur. Jade held perfectly still throughout, her black almond-shaped eyes wide and trusting.

Fascinated, Grant watched as Molly patiently instructed Katie on how and where to brush, and Katie followed her guidance to the letter. At one point, Molly put her arm around the girl's slender shoulders to steady her as she moved the brush farther down Jade's body. As they brushed, Katie's eyes shone with joy.

And so did Molly's. In fact, with her mouth curved into a gentle smile and her affectionate gaze on Katie, she looked more beautiful than he'd ever seen her. Both inside and out.

Grant couldn't look away, could barely draw a full breath around the lump of pure admiration and awe clogging his throat.

Molly Kent was something else, all right. Special. Rare. And very, very appealing. And thanks to her, he was beginning to understand that helping other people was worthwhile. Important. Validating.

What an incredible woman.

Just then, Molly shifted her gaze from Katie to him. Her green eyes snagged on his, holding, and her smile softened, morphing, if possible, into one of profound contentment and serenity. It was as if she was right where she belonged, here with Katie and him, bringing sunshine and happiness into the little girl's life.

Unable to fight Molly's draw, he smiled back, feeling her mental touch as if she had actually put her hand on his heart and squeezed.

Molly nodded slightly, as if she understood everything he was thinking. All at once, an unmistakable connection sparked, setting his heart rate zinging into the megawatt zone.

And all of a sudden, his deadline didn't seem like the most important thing in his life any longer.

Chapter Twelve

"Do you think Grant's coming?" Neil asked Monday evening as he set down a bowl of potato chips on the coffee table in front of Molly.

Her heart did a funny little bounce at the mention of Grant's name. "I'm not sure. I reminded him about the game when we took Jade to visit the kids at the hospital on Friday. But he was pretty noncommittal, and I know he's awfully busy...."

"Too busy for football?" Neil asked with an incredulous lift of his gray eyebrows, then whistled as he sat in the brown leather recliner next to Molly. "He must have some really pressing work to pound out if he's gonna miss this game. I didn't see him at church yesterday, either." He picked up Coco and set her on his lap. "Wonder why not?"

Molly knew why not, but it wasn't her place to share with Neil the problems Grant was having with his relationship to God. "I know he's on a very tight deadline."

Neil harrumphed. "I guess so," he said, sounding slightly offended. "Must be pretty important to miss all this fun."

Must be.

Seemed a bit odd, though. Call her crazy, but a bond had seemed to form between her and Grant as they'd looked at each other in Katie's room.

Maybe she'd imagined the whole exchange at the hospital. Or perhaps she was still emotionally off-kilter from the tense phone conversation she'd had with her dad yesterday; talking to him had always been stressful, especially since he had started making noises about wanting to see her.

Whatever the case, save for dropping off Jade and picking her up every day, Grant didn't seem to be inclined to seek Molly out, or spend time with her and Neil today. So be it.

She had her life, Grant had his, and he'd made no bones about wanting zero social life while he was in town. His motives were easy to see. Should be straightforward to deal with, given she wanted the same thing as far as romance went.

However…there was no way she'd dreamed his thrilling kiss on the beach. That had been as real as could be, and it hadn't been far from her mind since it had happened. She simply could not forget how wonderful it had felt to be in his arms. To have his attention and care for those few perfect moments.

Trying to put memories of Grant's kiss from her mind, she said to Neil, "Don't take it personally. Grant isn't really that hot on having a social life."

Neil picked up the remote and turned on his gargantuan flat-screen TV. "Mark my words, Moll. He's going to regret his choice later on."

She swallowed, a rogue thought crashing in on her.

I think he'll regret his choice, too.

Just then, the doorbell rang.

She looked at Neil. "Are you expecting anyone else?"

He shrugged. "Just Grant."

Her tummy dipped in an unmistakable yet completely ridiculous way. She rose. "It's probably just someone selling something," she said, scooping up Coco as she walked by. "I'll go see."

She headed to the door and opened it. Her heart just about stopped when she saw Grant standing there in a very nice brown leather bomber jacket, a grocery bag in his hand.

"Am I on time for the kickoff?" he asked, his eyes sparkling.

Explosions went off in her stomach. She stepped back, unabashedly thrilled he'd decided to come, after all. "You're just in time."

He walked in. "Good." He held up the bag. "I stopped and bought football food."

She raised a questioning brow as she closed the door behind him.

"Chips and dip," he said with a lift of his broad shoulders. "It's all I could come up with on the fly."

Her curiosity rose. "Were you in a hurry?"

"Honestly, until about twenty minutes ago, I wasn't even coming."

Her hopes took flight. "So you finished your project?"

"Oh, no. I'm not even close. I just needed a break."

Hope crashed and burned. Well, at least Grant recognized the need for some downtime, which her dad never had. "Been working hard, then?"

"Of course," he replied with a tilt of his head. "It's what I do."

"So you've said." He'd already worked more hours in the week since she'd met him than she did in double the time. How he did it without collapsing was beyond her.

"Neil will be glad you're here," she added. And so was she. Go figure.

"That's another reason I decided to come. I didn't want to disappoint Neil," Grant said. "I thought watching the game would be more fun for him in a group." He hoisted the grocery bag into his arms. "Besides, he reminds me of my dad, whom I've been missing a lot lately."

Something went all mushy and warm inside her. She loved it when the kind, considerate, vulnerable Grant shined through, erasing a part of the all-work-and-no-play machine he strived so hard to be. He seemed so much less like her dad when he was like this.

Not quite sure what to do with that eye-opening thought, she gestured to him to follow her. "Well, I'm sure he'll appreciate you taking the time to stop by."

"I'm not just stopping by," he said. "I'm staying for the whole game, even if the Seahawks are losing."

"Good!" she replied, meaning it. A whole evening spent with her two favorite men. Pretty wonderful.

Neil waved enthusiastically when they walked into the room. "Grant, my man. You decided to come!" He started to rise.

"Don't get up." Grant walked over and held out his free hand. "How's it going, sir?"

Neil shook his hand, staying put. "Great! Nothing like some football, some good company and some red-hot homemade chili simmering on the stove." He sucked in a huge breath, presumably to take in the smell of chili in the air, then his eyes fell on the grocery bag in Grant's hands. "Whatcha got there?"

"Just some chips and dip. Nothing fancy," Grant replied.

"Good," Neil said. "We don't like fancy food when we watch football, do we, Molly-girl?"

"No, we sure don't." She put a wiggly Coco down on Neil's lap. "I'll take them and put them in a bowl."

Grant held out the bag, and when she reached for it, she touched his hand in the process. She looked up at him, meeting his steady blue gaze.

He winked.

Her heart snagged a beat or two, and little tingles spread through the rest of her. Memories of his kiss danced through her brain like an enchanted dream, and one by one she felt the bricks on the wall around her heart begin to crumble.

Determined to just go with the flow tonight, she smiled at him and winked back, liking their nonverbal, private communication. After a second or two, she managed to look away from his pointed stare and make her feet carry her into the kitchen.

As she looked around for a bowl, she noted how odd it was that the giddy feelings, recollections of Grant's kiss and the knowledge that the wall around her heart was being threatened didn't scare or rattle her quite so much.

In fact, she loved the goose bumps his touch

gave her and the undeniably pleasant glow memories of his kiss stirred.

The wall-falling thing still scared her—opening herself up was a big step. But try as she might, she couldn't seem to convince herself her change in attitude was a bad thing at all.

Oh, boy. Was she in over her head or what?

Shockingly, tonight she couldn't seem to work up the fortitude to care.

At halftime, Neil went into the kitchen to serve up the chili, insisting that Molly stay put and keep Grant company. She agreed; it was obvious Neil was taking cues from her and turning into something of a matchmaker. Not bad for a rookie.

Butterflies danced in her tummy.

She looked at Grant sitting on the couch next to her. He'd taken off his coat and wore a dark brown long-sleeved, button-down collared shirt that coordinated nicely with his dark-washed jeans. He looked relaxed and settled in, completely content to be watching the game instead of burning the midnight oil at his computer. Of course, his seemingly mellow demeanor could be because the Seahawks were leading twenty to seven.

Or maybe it was because he was really enjoying his downtime. Probably it was a combination of both.

Whatever worked for him.

He took a swig of his soft drink, then looked at her. "How are you doing?"

She fidgeted, then studied Coco's fur. "I'm okay."

Grant leaned over and tried to catch her eye. "Is something wrong?"

She drew in a shocked breath at the sight of him sitting there, looking at her with what appeared to be concern gleaming from his blue eyes. He was perceptive, she'd give him that. When was the last time someone had actually wanted to be there for her? Well, someone besides Phoebe?

Someone of the male persuasion?

All at once, the need to talk to someone about the situation with her dad overwhelmed her. Grant was a smart guy. Brilliant, in fact. Maybe he could help her figure out what to do. At the very least, it would feel good to unload. Maybe vent a teensy bit.

She cleared her throat. "Nothing's wrong, exactly. It's just that…well, my dad called yesterday, and he wants to see me."

"Oh, wow." Grant leaned over and took her fingers in his, engulfing her hand in warmth. "You want to talk about it?"

She nodded, holding on to his hand, hearing Neil banging around in the kitchen. Working up her courage, she said, "Yeah, I guess I do."

Grant turned so he was facing her. "Shoot."

Pushing her hair behind one ear, she settled Coco more firmly on her lap and began. "Well, you know my dad and I are estranged."

"Yes."

"Until he started calling a few months ago, I hadn't talked to or heard from him in three years."

"Okay. Go on," Grant said reassuringly.

"So, he wants to see me, and, well…" She let out a shaky breath. "I'm just not sure I can do that."

Grant's eyes softened. "Because you haven't forgiven him for abandoning you."

A lump formed in her throat. "Right. And I know through my prayers that I need to forgive him to be able to move on with my life, but truthfully, I don't know how."

His arm slid around her shoulders and he squeezed gently. "You and I are a lot alike, you know."

"How so?" she asked, fighting the need to burrow into his embrace and stay there, safe and protected, for the next few years. Instead, she laid her head on his shoulder, feeling his warmth and support sinking into her even so, soothing her like a warm, healing balm.

"You don't know how to forgive your dad, and I don't know how to forgive God."

"I don't think I'd put my dad on par with God."

She quirked a lopsided smile. "Still. We're quite the pair, aren't we?"

An equally crooked, kind of secretive smile that made her feel truly special passed over his lips. "We sure are."

"So what do you think I should do?" she asked, furrowing her brow. "I could really use some advice."

Pausing, he blew out a breath, then sat back, taking her with him. Coco, bless her little heart, went along for the ride, and settled on the couch next to Molly. "Well, as someone who's very close to his dad, I guess I'm all for a person doing their best to find a way to forgive family if possible."

She nibbled the inside of her cheek. "I agree in theory. But what if he hasn't changed? What if he abandons me again? I'm not sure I can handle that."

"I guess that's the risk you take," Grant replied quietly. "But with risk also comes reward. Maybe he's really changed, maybe he's learned from his mistakes. Maybe he's capable of having a healthy relationship with you. Wouldn't that be great?"

She slowly nodded, knowing on some level that he spoke the truth, even though following his advice scared her to death.

Grant went on. "But how will you know if you don't open the door a crack?"

"Good point." Something occurred to her, and

she regarded him with a direct gaze. "Do you realize that I could turn this conversation around and say exactly the same thing about your inability to forgive God?"

Grant blinked.

"I mean, how do you know if you can trust Him if you don't give Him a chance?" she asked.

Grant's jaw worked. Then his face relaxed and he leaned over and gave her a quick yet tender kiss that made her lips tingle. "You're right," he said, his forehead touching hers. "Looks like we both have lessons to learn, doesn't it?"

"I guess so," she replied, loving being so close to him. "I'll try if you do. Somehow it seems easier to take scary steps if you have someone to help and commiserate with."

"It's a deal," he said, nodding emphatically. "Commiseration is always good."

"Does that mean you'll come to the Christmas Eve service with me at the end of the week? I can't think of anyone else I'd rather go with." She quirked her mouth. "Except Neil. Hope you don't mind if he tags along. I'd hate for him to be alone."

Grant drew in a long, shaky breath. "My mom loved Christmas."

Pushing back, Molly laid a hand on his rough jaw, her throat tightening with emotion. "I know it's hard to go through the holidays without her, but I think you'll really feel better if you go. Praising the Lord can be very healing."

He didn't respond, and his gaze fell.

Obviously, he wasn't ready to face a house of worship yet. Hopefully, he'd change his mind in the four days until the service on Friday. "Will you promise me you'll at least think about coming to church with me?"

After a pause, he said solemnly, "I promise."

She caressed his cheek. "Good."

Silence reigned for a moment, and then Neil called from the kitchen, "Chili's up, gang. Come and get it before I eat all of it."

"Sounds like the chow is ready." Grant stood, then took Molly's hand and helped her up from the couch. "Are you feeling better now?" he asked, his eyes shining with a caring glow that lightened her load tremendously while also making her feel as if she had someone to lean on—for a while— rather than being the one providing support. She liked the feeling.

"I am." Acting on pure impulse, she slid her arms around his waist and hugged him close.

His arms came down firmly around her, cocooning her against the beating of his heart. "Good. I don't like seeing you upset."

His words made her chest tighten. "Thank you so much for listening. I feel very fortunate to have you on my side."

He pulled back and ran a gentle finger down her cheek, holding her gaze. "It goes both ways, you know."

She nodded. "I know. Maybe we both need someone more than either of us really realizes."

"Maybe we do," he said, sweeping her hair back from her face, moving closer.

The sound of Neil loudly clearing his throat from the doorway broke the spell. Molly and Grant jumped back in unison.

"I hate to break this little lovefest up, but time's a-wasting, and if we want to eat before halftime's over, you two better get in here."

Molly giggled, then saluted Neil. "Aye, aye, Captain Neil. We're on our way."

Grant rubbed his hands together. "Show me the chili, fast. Suddenly I'm starving."

"Me, too," said Molly. And she didn't even like chili that much.

What in the world did that mean?

In the middle of the night, after the game at Neil's, Grant sat at his computer trying to work but failing miserably.

All he could think about was how much he'd enjoyed being with Molly today, holding her, talking, sharing. And the feel of her nestled in the crook of his arm, her fresh, flowery scent teasing his nose…well, he couldn't remember the last time he'd felt so good.

He pressed a hand to the bridge of his nose. Well, actually, he could remember. Jenna had made him feel the same way, all happy and content and complacent. And he'd poured himself into their relationship, so in love with her he could barely breathe, to a point where he'd bombed out of graduate school that semester, only to have her dump him for being a failure.

With his job on the line, did he really want to go there again, with Molly?

He wasn't sure he did.

Worse yet for his focus, he simply could not get their conversation about God out of his head.

Everything she'd said about forgiving Him made perfect sense. How, indeed, could he possibly hope to regain his faith if he didn't at least open the door for God? Because he knew now, thanks to Molly, that he *did* want to find his lost faith. Problem was, he didn't know how to trust again.

Finally, he pushed away and stood, frustrated by his lack of concentration. He stretched out the crick in his neck, then he put his hands on his hips and stared out the rain-speckled window, unable to see anything of the ocean save for some blurry white lines where the waves broke on the beach a hundred yards or so away.

He paced the dark house then, searching his mind for answers, his own words swirling through his brain.

But with risk also comes reward.

Did he really believe that? Yes, he did; he wouldn't have said it to Molly if he didn't believe it was true in the very core of his soul. He genuinely thought that was what she needed to focus on as she faced the challenge of forgiving her father.

How could he ask any less of himself?

So maybe he did, as she'd said, need to take his own advice. He needed to open the door, or God wouldn't find His way past the barriers Grant had mortared in place the day his mom had passed away.

He heaved out a shuddering breath, preparing himself to do something he hadn't done since his mother lay dying before him. Closing his eyes, he brought his shaking hands together in front of himself and sent up words to heaven.

Dear Lord, I know we haven't talked in a while. But I've been given some advice from a really wise, wonderful woman, and she's helped me to realize I need You more than ever right now....

Chapter Thirteen

On Christmas Eve, Molly sat beside Neil in the sanctuary of the Moonlight Cove Community Church, her hands clasped in her lap. The joyful sound of the choir singing Christmas carols filled the large high-ceilinged room.

Every time someone walked by, she glanced right, hoping it was Grant. She'd like to turn around but didn't want to seem *too* anxious, and she certainly didn't want to appear rude by rubbernecking the other parishioners.

Neil pressed his hand to her arm. "Don't worry. He'll show."

She looked at the empty space she'd left on the pew next to her, right by the aisle so Grant wouldn't have to disturb anyone to sit down. "I know," she said, even though she didn't know any such thing.

She hadn't seen hide nor hair of Grant since the

football game at Neil's, except when he'd dropped off Jade every morning and picked her up every evening. And she noticed that he'd seemed kind of subdued and distant then. So much so that she hadn't asked him about coming to church tonight.

Grant had made his wishes clear by staying away, and she needed to listen to what he was saying. Besides, he was leaving when Rose and Benny returned. And then he'd walk out of her life whether she wanted him to or not.

Might as well prepare herself now.

She heard the sanctuary doors close, and her heart sank. He wasn't going to show.

Fine. She could handle whatever happened.

Just as she'd given up hope and focused on the pastor and candle-lighters filing onto the altar, she felt something brush her sleeve.

She looked up and saw Grant sliding into the seat beside her. Her heart tripped, and happiness moved through her in a warm, swelling tide. He wore a dark charcoal suit, white dress shirt and cornflower blue tie that did wonderful things for his eyes.

As he flashed a gleaming smile, he briefly squeezed her arm.

"You made it," she whispered. Coming tonight was a big step for him.

He nodded, settling in beside her. "Yup. I decided my mom would have wanted me to come."

Her heart melted. "Ah. Good for you," she replied. "I think you'll really get something out of the service." It was important to her that he find as much comfort in God as she did.

Pastor Goodrich asked the congregation to rise. He offered a prayer, and Molly bent her head and closed her eyes, saying her own silent entreaty to God to help her find the strength and wisdom to forgive her father. Talking with Grant about his struggles to forgive God had made her realize the importance of repairing her relationship with her dad.

As the service went on, she couldn't help but like having Grant sitting next to her as the pastor delivered his sermon. The steady, warm pressure of Grant's leg against hers made her feel so secure, so content.

So…confused.

The praise band started playing and everyone stood to sing. The feeling of lifting her voice in praise to the Lord, along with Grant's remarkably good baritone ringing out beside her, made her wish he'd be beside her at every church service, forever.

Talk about a foolish dream.

The service ended with the church youth— including Katie, in a wheelchair—reenacting Christ's birth in Bethlehem. Molly slid a glance Grant's way as the skit played out on the altar.

With rapt attention, he watched the adorable kids up on stage act out the miracle of Jesus's birth. She heard him chuckle with everyone else when one of the kids flubbed her lines and had to be reminded of the correct line by the youth pastor standing in the wings.

Pride swelled through her; he was obviously really taking in the service, giving God another chance—or at least considering it—or he wouldn't have come. Wouldn't it be great if coming to church helped him down the road to having faith in God again?

The service ended with the Lord's Prayer, and then Pastor Goodrich's hearty wish for a merry Christmas and a happy New Year. Everyone stood and began to file out as the choir sang "Angels We Have Heard on High" accompanied by the band.

Grant stepped aside to let her and Neil out, then fell in step beside them, his hand a warm, steadying presence at the small of her back.

They arrived in the church foyer, where the congregation had gathered to chat. Neil excused himself to go talk to someone by the doors.

Molly turned to Grant. "So, what did you think of the service?"

"It was nice." His eyes reflected a suddenly somber light. "My mom would have loved it."

"I'm sure she would have," Molly said, fighting

the urge to take his hand in hers. "Did the worship make you feel closer to God?"

His expression grew decidedly wary. "In some ways," he said. "I...actually prayed the other night."

"How did that go?" she asked, excited by this news.

"All right," he replied, tilting his head to the side briefly. "For the first time in a long while, I feel as if I might be able to let God back into my life."

"That's great," she said truthfully. "I'm really happy for you." No matter what, she truly believed that Grant's life would be enhanced by reestablishing ties with the Lord.

Neil returned. "What do you say we go get some ice cream and hot chocolate at I Scream for Ice Cream?" he asked, rubbing his hands together. Neil adored ice cream.

Sounded like the perfect scenario to Molly, dessert and her two favorite men, enjoying Christmas Eve.

But...wait a second. Grant's presence in her life was temporary at best, and he hadn't made any promises. She had to be smart. Careful. Realistic.

Time to reel herself in.

Before she could do any reeling, Grant said, "So have you forgiven Phoebe for meddling?"

"Sure have. We talked a few days ago and straightened everything out."

Phoebe had been mildly apologetic for her scheme to get Molly and Grant together over meatloaf, after she'd pointed out that she had only been doing what Molly did on a regular basis under the guise of "matchmaking."

Molly had had no choice but to accept Phoebe's apology and eat some crow; Phoebe had spoken the truth. And really, Molly didn't mind acknowledging that Phoebe was right; ensuring that it was all good between her and her best friend was all that mattered.

"Good, good," Neil said eagerly. "I told her we might stop by before she closes. I really want some of that delicious candy cane ice cream."

"Sounds good to me," Grant replied. "You can never go wrong with ice cream."

But Molly could go wrong with Grant. Very wrong. Keeping that in mind, she said, "Don't you think you should get back to work?"

Grant frowned. "It's Christmas Eve."

"I know. But you have a deadline, right?" She pointed at her watch, then patted it. "Tick-tock."

Grant rocked back on his heels. "I guess you're right. I really *should* get back to work." He pressed a warm hand to her arm. "Merry Christmas, Molly."

She smiled the smile of her life, nodding amiably. "You, too."

Grant blinked, then turned and shook Neil's hand. "Take care, Neil."

"I will, Grant. You do the same."

With a lump in her throat, Molly watched Grant walk away.

And doggedly forced herself to remember that this was the way it had to be.

Grant went straight home from the service and got right to work, trying to put Molly from his mind by jamming all of his mental energy into his computer code.

But the fact remained, he couldn't forget how good it felt to sit next to her at the service, as if they were a couple worshipping together.

And during the game at Neil's…well, Grant couldn't deny that he'd enjoyed getting cozy with Molly while they discussed their problems.

And man, had her advice helped. Going to church had been wonderful. He'd really enjoyed the service, even though it had made him miss his mom so terribly he ached. Still, it had felt good to spend some time in God's house after being away so long. Cleansing. Calming. Healing. He had Molly to thank for that.

Molly. She was an amazing woman.

So what was he doing here, alone on Christmas

Eve, when all he could think about was a pretty redhead with gorgeous green eyes?

He had no idea. On impulse, he powered down his computer and stood.

Sure, Molly had cut their evening short and sent him home to work, and he sensed that something was wrong there, that something was bothering her. All the more reason to seek her out and talk.

Because, good or bad, tonight just didn't seem like a night to be by himself.

Chapter Fourteen

Humming along with "Silver Bells," Molly stood back and admired her decorating masterpiece, making sure all of the ornaments on her tree were placed just so. She made a few adjustments so all of her favorites were on the front of the tree, in full view. Better. Perfect, actually, in all of its Christmassy splendor.

"What do you think, guys?" she asked Peter and Parker, who were snoozing on the floor by the couch. Nobody responded. Not even a tail wag or lifted head after all her hard work. Lazy mutts. Good thing they were cute.

"Looks great, if I do say so myself, even if you guys aren't noticing."

She'd been so busy with the Christmas rush at Bow Wow Boutique, she'd almost forgone putting up a tree this year. But in the end, she'd decided that it just wouldn't be cool not to have one. She'd snagged the last decent tree on the lot just this morning, and had actually really enjoyed spending the evening decorating, with Christmas music playing in the background, the smell of cider simmering on the stove and the scent of sugar cookies baking in the oven.

She'd been in a little bit of a funk, though, since she got home from the church service; watching Grant leave had really socked her in the heart.

Better now than later as far as she was—

The doorbell rang, interrupting her thoughts.

Peter and Parker went from dead sound asleep into full bark mode in a nanosecond. They scrambled to the door, practically knocking each other over in their eagerness to be the first one there.

"Okay, okay," Molly said, chuckling. "I hear it, guys."

She headed over to the door, expecting to find some carolers on her porch, or maybe Mrs. Silner from next door delivering some of her famous cashew brittle. She hoped her visitor was Mrs. Silner. Carolers were great, but candy…way better.

Shooing the dogs back, Molly opened the door. And almost fainted when she saw Grant standing there in the clothes he'd worn to church, looking as good as he usually did.

Imagine. Grant here, instead of holed up on a hot date with his computer.

"Hey, you," she said, having the presence of

mind to block the door with her body so the dogs wouldn't attack Grant with paw bonks and slobbery dog kisses. "What's up?"

He shoved his hands in the pockets of his leather jacket, shifting on his feet. "I was hoping you'd be here. Can I come in?"

Her heart sped up. "Sure," she said, stepping back but still managing to keep the dogs in. She just didn't have it in her to turn him away again.

As soon as he stepped through the door, she closed it. The dogs went nuts at Grant's feet.

"Sit!" Molly shouted as she dug in her pocket for a treat. Amazingly, both dogs instantly dropped to a sit. She gave Grant a sheepish look. "Sorry for yelling."

She looked down at the canine pair, their coal-black eyes now trained on the person with the treats. "Good dogs," she said, handing out minute bits of chicken liver jerky.

"I see you follow your own advice with the dogs," Grant said. "They couldn't sit fast enough."

She cleared her throat, shocked yet very, very pleased Grant was actually standing in her entryway. Fighting his pull was impossible.

But…she shouldn't be so exceedingly glad to see him. "I only give advice about things I know something about." She patted her pocket. "Never underestimate the power of smelly dog treats."

"Trust me, I won't."

An awkward silence ensued.

Speak. She needed to speak instead of standing there like an idiot. "Um…would you like some mulled cider? I made it myself." When in doubt, or stunned stupid by a good-looking blue-eyed guy in a leather coat, offer refreshments.

"That sounds great."

"Let me take your coat, and we can go into the kitchen for cider."

He took off his coat and handed it to her. "Thanks."

As she folded the coat over her arm, the scent of his spicy aftershave wafted up from the warm garment, teasing her nose, sending tingles through her blood. Feeling her tummy flip and her cheeks heat, she did her best to act calm as she opened the closet door in the entryway and hung up his coat.

She headed to the kitchen through the living room and he followed.

"Hey," he said. "Your tree looks really nice."

"Thanks. As soon as we get our cider, you can help me light it up."

They went into the kitchen and grabbed mugs of steaming cider, then returned to the living room.

Afraid she'd spill cider all over her freshly cleaned carpet because her hands were trembling, she put her mug down on a coaster on the coffee table, then gestured to the couch. "Why don't we sit."

Grant followed suit, then sat on one end of the small couch and she sat on the other. The dogs plopped down by the Christmas tree.

"So. What made you quit working so early?" she asked. "You said you weren't anywhere near to meeting your deadline."

He shrugged. "I guess I just didn't want to be alone on Christmas Eve."

Hmm. That was a pleasant surprise. Maybe the human working machine had a shut-off switch, after all. "I can understand that," she replied, softening a bit. "It's lonely for us singles during the holidays." Maybe that was why she'd greeted him with open arms, so to speak.

"Yeah, well, the thing is, I'm not usually lonely at Christmas."

Interesting. "Do you usually spend the holiday with your dad?"

"In the evening, yes."

"But during the day?"

Grant took a sip of cider. "I work."

Not surprising. "So it's all about punching the time clock, isn't it?"

His jaw flexed as he looked askance at her. "Hence your *tick-tock* remark at church."

"Hey, you said it first, bucko," she said, raising a brow along with her mug of cider. "You live your life on a deadline."

"So what if I do?"

"Well, if living that way works for you, great." She shook her head. "But I grew up with my dad being on constant deadlines, and that's not what I want in my life." She looked at Grant, suddenly curious. "Have you always been this obsessed with work?"

He sat back, cider mug in hand. "Not always. But I've already told you I did study a lot in high school."

"Because?" she asked, wanting to understand him better.

He thought for a moment. "I'm not sure."

Remembering something, she said, "Didn't you tell me you went to your high school reunion as a successful, good-looking businessman who'd shed his geeky high school shell?"

He chuckled, and then seemed to blush slightly. "I don't recall saying anything about being handsome."

She deadpanned him. "Well, assume that you were." And still was.

Cocking his head in acknowledgment, he said, "Then, yes, I did go to my reunion feeling successful."

"So, did that float your boat?"

He flushed. "Truth?"

"Of course."

"It sure did."

She chewed on that for a few seconds. Respect. Acceptance. He didn't get any of either in high school....

Before long, the probable truth about Grant's motivations dawned on her.

Raising a brow, she said, "Is that why you're so driven now? Are you trying to capture the respect you never had in high school?"

He fiddled with his mug for a few seconds. Then he raised his blue-tinged gaze to her.

She couldn't look away. Could barely even draw a breath. Shaking a bit, she waited for his answer, sensing in some deep part of herself that his response could have the power to rock her world; if he had a good reason for his crazy work habits, a good rationale for being so much like her father... well, what then?

Wouldn't that be one less reason to keep him at a distance?

Lord, I need You. Now more than ever.

With bated breath, she waited for Grant's answer.

"Probably," he admitted in a soft, low voice, continuing to stare at her before he dropped his gaze. He shrugged, looking abashed. "What can I say? I guess I crave respect."

A lump formed in her throat, and part of the ice around her heart melted. Her well-shored, carefully built defenses fell that much more. Until they felt as if they were absolutely minute.

Gone...

Suddenly, an odd smell hit her nose. Something was burning....

"Oh, no!" she said, jumping up. "My cookies!"

She ran into the kitchen, the dogs hot on her heels, and yanked the oven open. There, in all their burned splendor, were her wreath-shaped cookies. Black ones.

She grabbed an oven mitt, yanked the cookie sheet out and threw it on the stovetop with a clatter. Pulling the mitts off her hands, she jabbed the button that turned the oven off and flipped the hood fan on.

Grant appeared in the arched entryway to the kitchen. "Overcooked?"

She huffed. "Burned beyond all recognition."

"Should we make another batch? I haven't decorated Christmas cookies since I was a kid. My mom loved to bake during the holidays."

"You sure it won't make you sad?"

"Not sure at all. In fact, I'm guessing it *will* bring on some sadness."

She gave him a questioning stare.

"But that's okay," he said. "I learned by going to church tonight that embracing the things my mom loved is comforting, and actually helps me deal with my sadness."

He'd come a long way in dealing with his grief. She liked to think she'd had something to do with his progress. "Well, great, then. I'll get the stuff out, and we can get started."

"First, though, you have to come here," he said, his eyes twinkling in a way that seemed very sly.

Tingles spread through her. "Why?"

"Just come over here for a second," he said, motioning toward himself. "I won't bite you."

"Okay." She walked over and stopped in front of him, getting close, but not too close. She was only human, after all. "What can I do for you?"

He looked straight up. "I do believe, Miss Kent, that we are now officially standing under mistletoe."

Following his gaze, she saw that he was right. How could she have forgotten that she'd tacked a piece of it in the kitchen doorway last week?

Her heart ka-boomed. Mistletoe could mean only one thing....

"Why, you're right, Mr. Roderick." She gathered her courage and put her hands on his shoulders, then pulled him down and whispered in his ear, "What in the world are we going to do about that?"

"Well, we have to follow tradition, you know," he whispered back in her ear as he slid his arms around her waist.

"Yes, of course," she said breathlessly. "It would be bad not to."

"Very bad," he replied, before his mouth caught hers in a tender, heart-tugging, stunningly perfect kiss.

Suddenly, baking cookies was the last thing on her mind.

An hour after he arrived at Molly's, Grant helped her light the tree, which, of course, involved replacing some burnt-out bulbs.

Then they turned off the lamps in the living room and settled onto the couch in the glow of the multicolored, twinkling tree lights. Their mugs of hot cider and the cookies they made when they'd finally stopped kissing under the mistletoe sat on the coffee table in front of them.

A distant voice told him he was getting in too deep, that he should back up and head home to his work. But the voice was just far enough away for him to ignore its weak prodding.

He couldn't remember when he'd felt so happy. So hopeful. What else mattered right now? Besides, it was Christmas Eve, the most wonderful night of the year. He deserved this break.

He tightened his arm around Molly's slim shoulders and pressed a gentle kiss to her sweet-scented hair. "I could get used to this."

Snuggling closer, she said, "Me, too."

"Listen, I want to thank you for encouraging me to go to church."

"I'm glad you liked the service."

"Don't get me wrong, it was rough. I missed my mom so much, I ached."

"I know that feeling." She grasped the hand he had hanging over her shoulder. "I'm sorry you had to go through that."

"No, no, don't be. Reconnecting with God felt really good." Wonderful, actually. "Kind of like I was coming home after being away too long."

"I thought that might be the case. Being close to the Lord has always been a great comfort to me."

"I didn't realize how much I'd missed my spiritual side, and my relationship with God."

She turned, then laid her warm hand on his cheek. "I'm so happy you've rediscovered those things."

Gazing into her fathomless green eyes, he admitted, "I really feel like my soul has begun to heal."

"You think?" she asked, a hopeful smile curving her lips.

"Definitely." He slid his arms around her and pulled her against his chest, unable to keep from closing the space between them. "And I have you to thank."

Just as he pulled away enough to kiss her sweet lips, the phone rang.

She put a finger on his lips. "Hold that thought."

Rising, she went into the kitchen and answered the phone. He could hear her voice murmuring, but couldn't make out the words. So he sat back and enjoyed gazing at the Christmas tree, even though his arms felt empty without Molly in them.

A few minutes later, she returned, her arms crossed over her chest, her expression grim.

Concern bubbled up. "What's wrong?" he asked, leaning forward.

"That was my dad." She sat on the very edge of the couch, her spine visibly rigid.

Grant reached out and rubbed her back. "And?"

She turned, and her eyes glittered with unshed tears. "He just got into town and wants to see me tomorrow."

"Oh, boy. You weren't expecting him, were you?" he asked.

Shaking her head, she replied, "Not at all. He's been calling a lot lately, and making noises about coming and seeing me…but I didn't expect him to just show up unannounced."

"What do you want to do?" Grant asked, reaching out and taking her hand to draw her to his side.

"I'm not sure I can face him." She wiped her eyes. "I'm still so…angry at him."

"I was angry with God, too."

"And you managed to start talking to Him again, didn't you?"

"Only after you pointed out that I needed to give Him another chance."

She remained silent for a long moment. "Why is it so much easier for me to see what other people should do, but not myself?"

"I don't know, but you're right." He traced circles around her upper arm. "I think this is one of those times when you need to take your own advice."

She took a deep, shuddering breath. "I guess I need to at least open the door or else I won't ever know if he's changed."

"Exactly. I know it's hard—believe me, I know. But I think you'll feel better once you've given him a chance."

She pulled back and looked at him, her eyes still misty. "Promise?" she asked in a small voice.

Touching his forehead to hers, he said, "I can't promise what your dad will do, or that he's actually changed. But I can promise that you'll feel much better knowing one way or another."

Her arms came up around his neck and she pulled him near. "Thank you for helping me through this. I don't know what I would do without you."

He held her close, his heart beating in perfect

time with hers. "I feel the same way. I could stay here forever."

Snuggling closer, she said, "Me, too."

His chest squeezed, and another voice echoed in his head.

How am I ever going to leave her behind?

Chapter Fifteen

After Grant left on Christmas Eve, Molly took his advice and called her dad back and agreed to meet. She suggested to him that they convene at the boutique the next day; she wasn't ready to have him at her house, but she wanted to be on her own turf for their discussion in case their heart-to-heart didn't go well.

So now, here she was at a quarter to twelve on Christmas Day, nervously straightening already straight shelves, awaiting the arrival of the father she deliberately hadn't laid eyes on in well over three years.

The father she'd never found a way to forgive.

She couldn't help but think about Grant as she methodically reorganized the dog collar display by color. She'd been so grateful for his presence last night, and for his candid, thoughtful advice. Honestly, if he hadn't been there, she would have completely freaked out when she'd found out her dad was actually *in* Moonlight Cove.

It had felt so good to have someone to rely on, to trust, to help her make a decision. And after Grant had found the courage to step back into a church to start reconnecting with God, shouldn't she at least be able to consider doing the same with her dad?

Sounded good, but the actual execution was proving dicey; she was a nerve-addled wreck. What if her dad came back into her life, and then cut out again? Just the thought of him abandoning her for a second time made her stomach clench. Made her want to lock the door and pretend he wasn't going to show up here in a few minutes.

She went back to her office, on the hunt for some chewable antacid. Once she found a roll, she chewed a few, then headed out front and stared out at a deserted, Christmas-bedecked Main Street without seeing much through the raindrops running down the window.

She chewed a fingernail, realizing as noon approached that she kind of wished she'd asked Grant to be here for moral support. Funny how he'd become her rock since he'd been in town. She really wasn't looking forward to the day he left.

That was an understatement. She was dreading his inevitable departure. Like it or not, he'd become very important to her in the last few days. More so than she'd ever imagined, or wanted, really.

She pressed her fingers to the bridge of her nose. How could she have let her guard down so easily?

She'd have to think about that burning yet loaded question, as soon as the situation with her dad was somewhat resolved. A girl could deal with only one emotional crisis at a time, and even one at the moment was a stretch for her. Two biggies? Wasn't happening.

She turned from the window, and just as she reached the counter, she heard the door open and the bells ring. Swallowing her trepidation, she turned.

Her father stood there, looking pretty much the same physically as she remembered him, with his tall, lean frame and close-cropped red hair he'd passed on to her, though his was now sprinkled with gray. But to her surprise, he was dressed in jeans, tennis shoes and a dark green sweatshirt from their alma mater, University of Oregon. She couldn't remember the last time she'd seen him in anything but his suit-and-tie work attire.

"Hey, Dad," she said, walking over to him. "Did you have any trouble finding the store?"

He shook the rain off his head. "No trouble at all. Moonlight Cove isn't that big."

"True."

Feeling awkward—he'd never been demonstrative, much less affectionate—she leaned in and gave him a slight hug. He hugged back, smelling just as she remembered—of Old Spice and the peppermints he kept in his pocket.

"How have you been?" he asked.

"Good, good," she replied. "Business is going well."

He glanced around. "This looks great."

"Yeah, I've worked hard to make this place what it is."

Nodding, he said, "I can see that."

Silence.

"Can you believe this rain?" he said after a while. "Hope there's no flooding."

She sighed. "Listen, Dad, let's just cut the small talk. I'm sure you didn't come here to discuss the weather."

"No, I didn't." He cast his gaze around. "Can we sit somewhere?"

Where were her manners? "Of course. Let's go back to my office."

He followed her back and sat in the chair angled into the corner next to her desk.

She sank down into her desk chair. "So." She crossed her legs, and fought not to cross her arms across her chest in the classic defensive stance, even though she was, out of habit, feeling pretty defensive. "Why did you need to see me?" No sense in putting off the inevitable. Whatever *that* was.

He nodded, then rubbed a hand over his jaw. "Well, the thing is…one of my partners in the firm dropped dead a month ago."

Compassion flooded her. "Oh, no, I'm sorry to hear that."

"Yeah, it was quite a shock." He cleared his throat. "So…I went to his funeral, and, well, there was hardly anybody there. His ex-wife had remarried, and he'd been so busy working, he had no kind of relationship with his kids."

A chill ran through Molly. "That's so awful." And, yet, so familiar. At least the relationship with his kids part.

She watched her dad's normally steady hands flutter over his thighs until he clamped down to still them. "Tell me about it. Going to that funeral got me to thinking, and I realized if I were to die today, I wouldn't have anyone at my funeral, either."

Sadness hit her hard. Unless he'd made some friends in the last few years, which it sounded like he hadn't, he was probably right. About most of it.

"I'd be there," she said truthfully. Blood was blood. "What kind of person doesn't go to their own father's funeral?"

"Yes, I'm sure you'd come." He laughed without humor under his breath. "But I'm not stupid enough to think you would be attending out of anything but duty."

She flushed, then looked at the floor for a moment. "That's not true." But, really, it was. Painfully so.

"Oh, come on, Molly. Don't blow sunshine around here. Not with me." He shook his head. "I've been a horrible father, and we both know it. I wouldn't blame you if you wrote me off forever."

Her jaw dropped, and all she could do was stare. Where were these insightful thoughts coming from? Her dad had always seemed like the least perceptive, least clued-in person she'd ever known.

"What?" he said, arching a brow. "You think I don't know what a terrible job I did as a dad?"

"I...I don't know what I think." Her mind was spinning off track; she was stunned by his unexpected confession. "I...guess I assumed you were clueless." She felt tears burning her eyes, and she closed them for a moment to try and stem the tide. When would her father stop having the power to hurt her?

When she quit letting him. Sitting up straighter, she said, "If you knew what you were doing, why in the world did you do it, then?"

He had the good grace to look deeply ashamed.

After a few beats, he said, "You know how much I loved your mother, right?"

She nodded, digging a fingernail into her palm to distract herself long enough to keep the tears at bay.

"Well, when she died..." He dropped his head, then looked up, his eyes glimmering. "A big piece of me died with her."

Molly drew in a shaky breath, her jaw quivering as empathy grabbed a hold of her. They had that in common.

"I was so lost, so heartbroken, so filled with grief...I could barely function," he confessed.

Molly nodded, clenching her hands together in her lap. "I knew that, Dad, and...I was sad, too, but I was too young to understand what was going on. I needed you, and you weren't there."

His face crumbled. "I know, I know." He reached out and grabbed her hand. "But the thing was, I had no idea how to cope with the loss myself, much less how to help you cope. The only thing that helped was working."

Pressing a visibly shaking hand to his forehead, he continued, "And every time I looked at you, I saw your mom, and my heart broke all over again. I felt so helpless, so powerless and so ill-equipped to handle the pain."

His words cracked her heart in two. Finally, Molly's tears crested and spilled over onto her cheeks. "I felt like I lost both my parents when Mom died," she said, her voice breaking. "I was in pain, too, and I had nowhere to turn."

"I know, and I failed you badly. I was the adult, and I should have been there for you."

His words soothed the hurt just a bit. "Yes, you should have."

"Can you ever forgive me?" he asked, his voice husky. Raw. "I don't want to die all alone. I want another chance, Molly. I really do."

Her chest clenched so tightly she could barely breathe. She looked at him through a veil of tears, seeing the anguish in his eyes, the sincerity shining through. He appeared truly regretful, truly sorry. And, after all, this was her father, her flesh and blood. Her only close family. How could she turn him down?

And how could she not practice what she'd preached to Grant about forgiveness? As he'd so wisely said, she needed to heed her own advice.

Another thought occurred to her; her dad had said he loved her mom so much, his grief had taken over when he'd lost her.

I would feel the same way if Grant were gone from my life....

A shiver ran up her spine. All at once, Molly understood what had caused her father to let his lost love take over. And the astonishing truth wrapped up like a wonderful gift in that realization knocked her flat.

She loved Grant.

Pressing a hand to her racing heart, she had to take a few breaths before she could speak. "Dad…I understand how a lost love could make a person do crazy things."

He blinked. Three times. "You do?"

"Yes. Because…there's a man named Grant who I've just realized I love very deeply." Irrevocably. An overwhelming yet ecstatic sense of wonder rolled through her.

Something melted inside, some frozen part she'd kept cold for a very long time. It had taken her falling in love to thaw the lump of ice housed in her heart, allowing her to empathize with her dad in a way she'd never been able to before.

Her dad smiled, his eyes soft. "He's a lucky man," he said. "Does he know?"

"No, not yet."

"Well, tell him soon," he replied, a hint of reproach in his voice. "You don't want to waste one minute of time letting him know."

"You're right," she said. "I'll tell him very soon." In the meantime, she'd have to give thanks to God for guiding her to being able to forgive her dad, and for helping her to realize that she loved Grant.

Gifts from the Lord? Definitely.

"Good." Her dad turned hopeful eyes to her. "And what about us?"

Grant's words from the Lord's Prayer echoed in her head.

Forgive us our trespasses as we forgive those who trespass against us.

A wondrous sense of calm, of serenity, came over her. She knew what she had to do. "I can forgive you," she said softly. "But I need you to promise you won't run away from me again."

"I understand," he said, smiling hesitantly. "I promise I won't shut you out again."

"Then, welcome to my life," she said. She stood and held out her arms.

He rose and gave her a bear hug. "This was more than I was hoping for. The best Christmas present ever."

"For me, too," she said, patting his arm. She pulled back. "Why don't we celebrate our reconciliation by spending Christmas Day at my friend Phoebe's house."

"You sure she won't mind if I tag along?"

"Nah, she'll be thrilled," Molly said. "Let's go so we don't miss the snacks."

"Is Grant going to be there?"

"No, he has to work." A niggling of unease ran through Molly as she said the words. Reality jolted her. Grant was incredibly driven and worked insane hours. But she told herself that her love was strong enough to accept Grant. As he was.

And that meant dealing with the possibility of a long-distance relationship, and the reality that, more often than not, work would come first with the man she loved.

On Christmas Day, Grant did his best to keep his head down and his thoughts clear of Molly so he could do some damage against his ever-tightening deadline. But his strategy wasn't very successful. It seemed as if his work had somehow had babies. Lots of them.

Even so, no matter what he did, how much he tried to lose himself in his code, all he could think about was a pair of lovely green eyes, and the wonderful redhead they belonged to.

Christmas Eve with her had been fantastic. Sitting there, with the tree lights glowing and soft carols playing in the background and Molly snuggled up beside him had been one of the most peaceful and awesome moments of his life. And the kissing, holding her close...well, all of it had been so unforgettable.

He'd have to manage to forget some of it, though, or at least put it out of his mind temporarily if he entertained any hope of keeping his job. Which he did.

And he'd somehow figure out what to do about

his growing feelings for Molly, too. Eventually. Facing the fact that he was falling for her—and dealing with it—while trying to concentrate on work wasn't in the cards.

One challenge at a time.

Just as he managed to get a pretty good string of hours under his belt, his cell phone rang.

He grabbed it, noting with concern that it was his boss calling. On Christmas Day. Must be urgent. "Hello?"

"Hey, Grant, it's Malcolm."

"Hi, Malcolm. What's up?"

An audible sigh came over the line. "I just got off the phone with Sidney Vickerson."

Sid was the IT Director for Jovell Industries, the company that had contracted Grant's firm, Brick Software Consultants. As in *the client*. "And?"

"He wants to move the timeline up."

Grant rubbed his gritty eyes. "The timeline is already incredibly tight."

"I know. But they need the work more quickly to make up for changes on the far end of their software go-live."

"I'm already working night and day to get this stuff done." Grant leaned back in his chair, stretching his legs out. "I'm not sure I can work any quicker." Probably best not to mention that some of his time had been spent with a pretty, sweet, incredible woman named Molly.

"I figured that, so I'm bringing in Jim Lewis to help you out."

Jim used to work with Grant but had left the company to start his own software consulting business. "Great. He's good. That'll help."

"The thing is, he'd only agree to the job if you two could work together here in Seattle. His mom's ill, and he needs to stay in town."

A rock landed in Grant's gut. "So you need me to come back."

"I do. And as soon as possible. Jim's set to start work tomorrow."

Conflicting emotions—sadness, resignation, a tinge of panic—rose in Grant. Words clogged his throat, and the only sound that came out was a frustrated grumble.

After a long silence, Malcolm spoke. "Grant, I don't need to tell you how important this job is to Brick, do I? This project alone will account for a huge portion of our revenue, and if we complete it on time, it will set us up to contract even more business from Jovell."

Grant knew the drill. He'd invented it at Brick, actually. But that had been before an amazing woman named Molly had come barreling into his life and worked her way under his skin so thoroughly, he'd actually blown off his deadline on too many occasions already to spend time with her.

Look where *that* strategy had gotten him.

"I know how important Jovell is to Brick," he said to Sid. But he'd forgotten since he'd met Molly, hadn't he?

"Then head back to Seattle and get to work," Malcolm said. "There's a big bonus and a promotion in it for you if you make this deadline."

Grant closed his eyes for a moment. He should be happy. He was on the brink of his much-dreamed-of career success and all the industry respect he'd ever want. This was what he'd worked so hard for, what had driven him for years.

What he'd always wanted.

He stared off into space for a few seconds. He had to make a choice.

Work had never let him down. But love…well, love had never been his friend.

He swallowed and pushed out, "I'll leave first thing in the morning." This was the way it had to be. The way it had always been.

The way he wanted it.

"Great," Malcolm said. "I knew I could count on you, Grant."

Grant hung up, his shoulders slumped. Yeah, he was the go-to guy, all right. The one who would work night and day, all in the name of the job. Why didn't that persona make him feel better as it always had? What was his problem?

He was losing it for sure. Good thing work was

his tonic, his remedy. Once he got back to Seattle and the insane schedule at Brick, he'd be just fine. He just needed time. And then…everything would be as it should.

Before he left town, though, he'd need to find Molly and tell her he was leaving Moonlight Cove. He owed her that.

Just the thought of the conversation made his chest ache, as if someone had taken a machete to his heart and cut it into little pieces. But with some distance and an obscene amount of work to distract him, his chopped-up heart would be whole again.

As usual, he was counting on his work to pull him through.

He only hoped it succeeded this time around.

After a huge, delicious Christmas dinner at Phoebe's, Molly headed home to let the dogs out. Her dad stayed at Phoebe's a while longer to socialize with Phoebe's dad, which Molly viewed as a very good sign that her dad was truly changing his ways. Normally he would have been hightailing it out of there as soon as possible to work, barely even staying long enough for dessert. Maybe there was hope for him yet.

Please, God, make it so. It would be great to have a father back in her life and actually present.

As she drove up to her house, she was surprised

and pleased to see Grant's car in her driveway. She pulled up next to his vehicle, her heart lifting, and turned off the ignition. He slowly climbed out of his car and waited for her.

Smiling a goofy grin, she jumped out of her car, eager to tell him her news.

"What a nice surprise," she said as she rounded the front of her car, ready to launch herself into his arms.

But instead of opening his arms, his hands remained shoved into his coat pockets. And it looked as if someone had pushed Pause and he was stuck in a sad scene in a movie.

Uh-oh. She slowed down and halted, high anxiety slithering through her veins like used motor oil. "Whoa, that's a somber face. What's wrong?"

"Let's go inside," he said. "It's chilly out here."

"Okay." On autopilot, she headed to the front door, her stomach flipping, pancake style. She unlocked the door and greeted the welcoming dogs. Grant followed her in, noticeably subdued.

Noticeably distant.

Dismay bubbled up, filling her with an impending sense of dread she couldn't shake.

As soon as she calmed the dogs down, she spun on Grant. The unknown was killing her, even though she had a feeling what she didn't know might hurt when she got the scoop. "Okay, spill. What's got you all long-faced and quiet?"

He let out a heavy breath. "Let's go sit."

Great. She needed to be seated for whatever he was going to tell her. Filled with an impending sense of alarm, she led the way into the living room.

Once they were seated on the couch, Grant said, "So…my boss called."

Her tummy dipped. "Okay."

"And…our client has moved up the deadline." He looked at the floor, then at her. "I have to go back to Seattle."

The bottom fell out of her stomach. "When?" she asked, her eyes tingling.

"First thing in the morning."

Nodding, she said woodenly, "That soon?"

"They're bringing in someone to help me, starting tomorrow."

Okay. She'd hit a bump in the road. It was no secret Grant was driven, and she understood why. His stance didn't change anything. She loved him. And she had to tell him. No matter how much doing so scared her more than anything else she'd ever faced. But she somehow sensed she'd regret it if she let him walk away without speaking up.

With her stomach knotted, she looked at him, then gave him a shaky smile. "The thing is…" Words stuck in her throat.

"Go on," he said quietly.

She forced herself to look at him, to draw

strength from the depths of his beautiful blue eyes, to remember what a wonderful, kind man he was, to keep in mind all of the things she loved about him. All of the reasons she wanted to be with him forever.

"I love you, Grant," she whispered.

Her words hung in the air, swirling like smoke.

Wide-eyed, Grant looked…stricken. Shocked. "Oh. Wow." He looked at the floor. "Um…I didn't expect this."

Unwanted tears threatened. "Yeah." She grimaced and let out a rough sound. "I can see that."

"I don't know what to say…" He rubbed his jaw. "Wow."

Another bump. Fine. "Say you'll stay here with me."

He rose and started pacing. "I can't stay," he finally said. "My job's in Seattle."

She'd anticipated that line. "Well, Seattle's not the moon, you know."

"You talking about a long-distance thing?" he asked, frowning.

"We could try it…?" Or maybe she could move to Seattle….

He sat and took her trembling hand in his. "Molly, you know that I'm not looking for a relationship."

She nodded. Again, no secret. "Yes. I wasn't,

either. But I fell in love, anyway." Squeezing his hand, she said, "With you."

He sat there for a long moment, silent.

Molly's heart pounded so loudly she could hear it, feel it going *thunkety-thunk* inside of her. Maybe now was the time to offer to try living in Seattle, with Grant. Pet stores were popular everywhere, weren't they?

Finally, he said, "I can't do this, Molly. I just… can't."

Her stomach caved in, hollowing her out. The Seattle offer? Maybe not. "You don't even want to try?" she asked, her chin quivering.

"It wouldn't work," he said, his eyes soft, but not soft enough to cushion the blow. "For me, work and romance just don't go together."

She nodded, unable to speak as she felt her heart break in two. Suppressing a gasp at the ache building in her chest, she pulled her hand from his.

After a long pause, he let out a breath. "I guess…this is goodbye."

The word seemed so final. So solemn. So… wrong. But…she wasn't going to beg him to stay any more than she already had. She knew from dealing with her dad that no one could be forced to love someone else.

Or stick around.

Grant had made his choice—his job. She'd have

to live with that choice, no matter how much it tore up her heart. "I guess it is."

He stood there for a moment, not saying anything. Then, before she could see it coming, he took her hand again.

She looked at him, holding back a sob, her lips quivering.

"Thank you for helping me find my way back to God. I couldn't have done it without you," he said, his eyes shining with sincerity and what looked like tenderness. "I hope you believe me about that."

Her throat tightened, making speech impossible. So she just moved her head up and down, her lips pressed together tightly.

With a squeeze of his hand, he rose and left her sitting there in her living room. She ruthlessly stifled the need to call him back with every ounce of resolve she could muster.

But then something important occurred to her. "Grant!" she called, standing.

He came back in. "Yes?"

Oh, how she wished he were coming back for real. For her. But that was a fantasy, not reality, and she had to accept the painful truth. "I think we've overlooked one detail in this scenario."

"What?" he asked, dipping his eyebrows.

"Jade."

"Oh, yeah. I…uh, forgot about her."

She sighed. He couldn't even commit to a dog. How hopeless was that?

"Would you mind keeping her until Rose and Benny get home?" he asked, looking as sheepish as he should given he was hightailing it out of his responsibilities.

Molly tightened her mouth, her mind hovering on her first instinct, which was to tell him he was on his own with Jade. But Jade shouldn't have to suffer because Grant couldn't—or wouldn't—stay. She was an innocent doggy bystander in the mess of her and Grant. "No, of course I don't mind."

"Thanks."

"You're welcome." She grimaced. "Bring her by before you leave tomorrow."

He nodded tersely, but didn't speak.

And then he was gone.

She heard the front door open, then close with a *clunk,* a final death knell for her hopes and dreams of finding a love that would last a lifetime. But for her, finding such a thing was as elusive as trying to pin down the wind blowing through the trees in her backyard.

Tears finally poured down her cheeks, and a low sob of anguish escaped her for the loss of a love she now realized she'd wanted more than anything else in the world. Her legs trembling, she sat back down on the couch.

Peter and Parker came over and, in tandem,

jumped up onto the couch, landing on each side of her. Peter lay his head on Molly's knee, and Parker followed suit. They both looked up at her with what seemed like sympathy shining from their coal-black eyes.

Obviously, they'd learned a thing or two about intuitiveness from Jade; they seemed to know when their person needed comfort.

With a sniff, Molly leaned over and put her arms around each of the dogs, burying her nose in Parker's fur.

And as her tears soaked Parker, Molly was sure her heart, her life, would never be the same again.

Chapter Sixteen

Despite her best efforts to keep herself out of any kind of funk, Molly spent the next few weeks deeply mourning Grant's sudden departure. She kept to her regular schedule at work, though, and made sure that, to outward appearances, she seemed fine.

But in reality, she was a mess emotionally, and cried herself to sleep every night. She felt hollow, empty, as if some vital piece of her had been carved out and carted away, permanently. She feared her heart would never heal, and didn't quite know what to do about the situation except hope that time would mend what ailed her.

But she had her doubts. This wound seemed permanent.

Rose and Benny returned on schedule just after New Year's. Even though Rose kept mum on how she felt, Molly could sense that the older woman, who'd become a hopeless romantic since she'd found love, was disappointed not only that Grant had taken off early, but that he and Molly hadn't "hit if off" as Rose had hoped.

Neil and Phoebe had both asked about Grant and why he'd left so suddenly. Needing to keep her hurt to herself, Molly had explained in very general terms why he'd left but hadn't told either one of them she'd fallen in love with Grant. Talking about the situation was just too painful, too tender.

A little over three weeks after Grant left, Molly was surprised to see her dad walk into Bow Wow Boutique one Friday afternoon just after lunch. And she was even more astonished to see he held a tiny white puppy in his hands.

"Oh, my goodness," she said, walking toward him. "You should have told me you were coming." Portland was over two hours away. Doable, yes. But still, a fairly significant drive.

"Yeah, but I wanted to surprise you," he said, holding up the puppy. "What better reason for a pre-weekend road trip?"

"Who do you have there?" she asked, unable to keep from smiling. Puppies always made her happy. Although, nowadays, not much lifted her spirits.

His face split into a goofy grin. "This here is Jojo."

Molly gently petted Jojo's silky head. "He is

absolutely adorable." She held out her hands and her dad placed Jojo in them. "Maltese?"

"Good eye. Yup. My neighbor's sister breeds them, and…well, I decided it was time to get a dog. And *he's* a *she*."

Molly gave her dad a dubious look, then cuddled Jojo up to her cheek, breathing in her sweet puppy smell. "You hate dogs."

"Why do you say that?"

"Because I always wanted one growing up, and you'd never let me have one."

"Oh. Well, yes. But it wasn't because I didn't like dogs. It was because I didn't have time for one."

"Aha," she said. "And now you do?"

"I told you. That guy in my company dying knocked some sense into me, and I'm determined to turn over a new leaf. I'm spending less time at work and more time at home with that little gal," he said, pointing at Jojo.

"Glad to hear it, Dad. I think you'll find life away from work is pretty nice. Especially with an adorable new puppy to keep you company."

"Well, I hope you don't mind if I visit you here in Moonlight Cove every once in a while."

Her heart warmed. "No, of course I don't mind. And it'll certainly be fun to have this pup in our lives."

"Where are your dogs?" he asked, glancing around.

"Asleep in the back room." She carried Jojo toward the door. "Let's introduce them."

Peter and Parker were extremely interested in the puppy, and each gently sniffed her when Molly put her on the floor. Jojo sniffed back, her tail wagging, and then, sensing in the way of dogs where the softest sleeping place was, immediately climbed up onto the dogs' corduroy bed and plopped down right in the middle. With a puppy sigh, she put her head down and promptly fell asleep.

"She's exhausted from the trip here," her dad said. "You mind if she sleeps there for a while?"

"Not at all. Let's leave the door open and head out front." Molly grabbed two bottles of water from the mini-fridge and handed one to her dad.

As they walked out front, Peter and Parker following at their heels, her dad said, "So, how're things going with you and Grant?"

Just the sound of Grant's name made Molly ache. She fiddled with some paperwork on the counter. "He left town."

"Why?"

Molly put her water bottle down on the counter. Maybe it was time to spill to someone. Holding it all in was wearing on her big-time. "Things didn't work out with him." She fiddled with some paperwork. "He left the day after Christmas."

Her dad put a comforting hand on her arm. "Oh, I'm so sorry. Did he say why he left?"

"His office needed him in Seattle."

Dad froze. "He could be me," he said in a monotone.

"The similarities hadn't escaped me," she replied dryly. "Seems I have a way of ending up with workaholics."

He winced.

"Sorry."

"No, no. I was a workaholic, no question." He propped a hip against the counter. "I deserved that."

"Well, work called, and he answered." Molly went over and straightened the collar display. "End of story."

"Did you tell him you love him?"

"Yes, I did." She sniffed. "Didn't matter. He didn't want to do long distance, and he didn't want to stay."

Dad moved closer. "Did you offer to move to Seattle?"

"No." She put down the pink-and-white-flowered collar she held and crossed her arms over her chest. "I was going to, but then he said he didn't want a relationship, and I nixed the idea. Besides, my business is here." And if she kept telling herself that Bow Wow Boutique was enough, eventually she'd believe it.

"And his business is there. How could you expect him to stay and sacrifice his job if you weren't willing to do the same for him?"

Understanding rolled through her. She'd been so hurt, so knocked flat by Grant's decision and departure, she hadn't even thought of that. Why had she expected so much of Grant, things she wasn't willing to do? She had to put more on the line.

And, even though he'd said he didn't want a relationship, she knew he'd felt something for her; she hadn't imagined that, she was sure. Was he just scared, and sticking to his old ways of protecting his heart by pushing her away?

Wasn't that what she'd done? So why should she blame him for doing the exact same thing?

She chewed on her cheek for a second as inevitable worries sprang up. "But what if he doesn't choose me, even if I say I'll move to Seattle?"

Her dad cocked his head. "Well, that's a risk you're going to have to take. But I think you should pursue every avenue possible."

Fear spread its insidious roots through her. She headed back over to the front counter and gathered up some stray items that needed reshelving. "I don't know if I can take being rejected again."

Her dad followed her. "Can you take living without him?"

"The last few weeks have been some of the saddest of my life." She gave a humorless laugh. "So I guess not."

"Then you have to leap, and worry about the consequences later."

Her heart started thumping, and her stomach dipped. "That's a pretty scary proposition."

"Yeah, I know," he said, shrugging. "But anything worth having is worth the risk."

She looked at him, amazed. "How did you get to be so smart when I wasn't looking?" she asked, impressed with the man her father had chosen to become.

"I got smart about love when I didn't choose my daughter a long time ago and regretted it with every bone in my body, that's how." He shook his head. "Trust me, I learned the hard way."

Warmth rushed into her chest.

He looked at her and continued on, genuine regret reflected in his dark green eyes. "Don't make the same mistakes I did, honey. You've got to fight for what you want, or accept being alone. And somehow, I just don't think that living without Grant—and accepting his decision without a fight—is a good option for you."

She drew in a deep, shuddering breath and dropped the items in her hands on the counter, fully accepting the truth and its frightening implications.

"Oh, my goodness, Dad. You're right," she said.

"I wasn't willing to make any sacrifices for love. But now...the thought of spending the rest of my days without Grant in my life fills me with an aching painfulness that just won't go away."

Her dad put his hands on her shoulders and squeezed. "Go fight for the man you love, or you'll regret it for the rest of your life."

She thought about what he had said. He made a lot of sense and had pointed out what she'd been too scared to acknowledge. She saw now that she'd let Grant go without much of a fight to protect herself, but had actually ended up devastated in the end, anyway. Protection? Ha! More like hiding her head knee-deep in sand.

At least if she fought harder for their love she'd know that she hadn't just rolled over and accepted his decision so she wouldn't have to take any real risk. Or, worse yet, know that she'd chickened out when the love of her life was on the line.

"Okay," she said, her stomach pitching. "I'll go to Seattle." She frantically looked around. "But how can I leave the store and the dogs...?"

Dad shooed her toward the door. "I'll hold down the fort here until closing. Just go, and don't worry."

She pulled him into a quick hug. "Thank you, Dad, for helping me to see what I needed to do."

"You're welcome, sweetie. Glad I could finally be here when you needed me."

"Me, too." It had been a long time since her dad had been there for her. Too long, actually. She was glad that part of her life was going well.

But how about the part with Grant? Would he return her love, or walk away again?

She'd never know until she truly leaped with both feet and put everything out there. She only prayed Grant would be there to catch her when she jumped.

Please, Lord, help me to handle whatever love has in store for me with grace and strength.

No matter what.

"Congrats, Grant."

From behind his desk, Grant looked up and saw his coworker Mike Clark standing in the open door to Grant's office. "Thanks, Mike."

"That's quite the award," Mike said, nodding to the engraved monstrosity of a plaque taking up a good part of the space on Grant's desk. "Employee of the Year always warrants the biggest, most ostentatious plaque ever."

Grant chuckled. "Yeah, I know. I'll probably hang it over there," he said, pointing to the empty space on the wall next to the window. "Only place it'll fit."

Mike waved goodbye, and Grant was alone. He gazed at his award, given to him at a luncheon earlier today, then ran his finger over his name, engraved in flowing script.

GRANT RODERICK
EMPLOYEE OF THE YEAR
BRICK SOFTWARE CONSULTANTS

And he felt…not much. Mild pride, yes. But nothing more.

Rubbing his eyes, he rocked back in his leather desk chair, waiting for jubilation to gush through him. Even a small dose of happy giddiness for being awarded his company's highest honor. He'd coveted this award for years. Had actually pictured the thing on his wall. Many times.

But…nothing remotely resembling happiness hit him. In fact, aside from a small amount of satisfaction for actually meeting, with Jim's help, the impossible deadline thrown at him, all he felt was a lingering sense of sadness he hadn't been able to shake since he left Moonlight Cove.

Since he'd left Molly.

He rose and looked out the window of the eighteenth-floor office he'd moved into yesterday. The corner office sported a killer view of the cloudy Seattle skyline and was one of the best offices at Brick, given annually to the recipient of the EOY award. The place was his for the next year, and a promotion and pay raise were already in the works.

He should be ecstatic. He'd arrived. He had in his pocket a position he'd had his eye on for a very long time. A place he'd worked day and night, literally for years, to reach.

And aside from a vague sense of relief that he'd pulled the Jovell job off without collapsing in a heap of exhaustion, securing the account for future years, he felt...nothing.

He frowned. This wasn't the way this moment was supposed to play out. This wasn't how he'd envisioned he'd feel when all of his hard work paid off and he had the accolades he'd wanted since he'd graduated from college.

Restless, he began to pace around his office, trying to figure out what was going on. Why was he feeling so dissatisfied with his life, so lonely and depressed? This was the same life he'd had before he went to Moonlight Cove, and he'd liked it just fine then. He'd had his job which he loved, a nice home and financial security.

But he hadn't met Molly yet. And since he had...well, nothing seemed the same. He missed her sense of humor, their conversations and the way she always made him think, the way she challenged him and encouraged him to help others. And it went without saying that he missed having her in his arms.

He even missed Jade.

It was becoming clear that the prospect of never

seeing Molly again seemed very, very wrong. Sure, he had a great job that he was good at, one that had sent loads of rewards his way. But since he'd returned, his job just hadn't seemed like enough. Something was missing since he'd left Molly behind. Something important.

He'd thought his need for tangible job rewards had accounted for his feelings of dissatisfaction. But he had those rewards now, and he was still feeling as if something just wasn't right. And he yearned for Molly so much he ached.

But was he ready to put a woman first in his life, above all else? He didn't do things halfheartedly; if he was going to commit to Molly, it would have to be forever and always. She deserved nothing less.

As he rubbed his face with his hands, he tried to assimilate his jumbled thoughts into some semblance of order so he could figure out what to do next.

Because he had a feeling whatever he decided would be life-changing and profound. In fact, it would be the most important decision he'd ever made.

Lord, can we talk?

The stakes had never been higher.

Molly called Rose before she left Moonlight Cove to get the name of the company Grant worked for in Seattle. Rose had happily supplied the information, and said she was glad Molly had "come to her senses" about Grant. Molly had laughed and said she was glad, too, then made Rose promise not to contact Grant to tell him Molly was coming. Rose grudgingly agreed.

Molly printed out directions and arrived at Grant's office in midafternoon, stiff from her three-hour drive in the intermittent rain. But she was also excited and energized to finally tell Grant that she loved him and would do anything to ensure they had a future. Including moving to Seattle. Or the moon. Whatever it took.

She took the elevator up to the eighteenth floor, her legs shaking. When she got out of the elevator, large glass doors inscribed with the words BRICK SOFTWARE CONSULTANTS in big gold letters greeted her. Taking a deep breath for courage, she opened the doors and stepped inside, impressed by the tasteful leather couches and dark wood furniture in the lobby.

An older woman with short gray hair and large glasses looked up from a flat-screen computer monitor behind the reception desk. "May I help you?"

Molly swallowed. "Yes. I'm looking for Grant Roderick."

"I'm sorry, Mr. Roderick has already left for the day."

Crushing disappointment spread through Molly. "Oh, no." She should have called, but she wanted to surprise him, and had figured she had a pretty good chance of finding Grant at work, given the schedule he usually set for himself. He didn't seem like the type to knock off early. Even on a Friday.

The older woman looked at her, one drawn-on brow raised. "Would you like to leave him a message?"

Molly shook her head. "No, that's okay." What she had to say was too private to be said in an interoffice note.

"Are you a personal friend of Grant's?" the woman asked.

"Um...well, yes."

"Then if you'd like to leave him a note in his office, you can." She pointed right. "He just moved into the last office on the right, down that hall."

"Thank you."

Molly made her way down the corridor lined with offices, noting that most of them still had people working in them, which highlighted how strange it was that Grant had left early.

She found Grant's corner office and walked in, noting at once the stunning view of Seattle spreading out before her. Wow. This was really something. Definitely prime office real estate.

She looked around, noting the bare walls and absence of any kind of personalized decor. Made sense if he'd just moved in. She took in his large dark wood desk, which was clear except for a gigantic plaque sitting smack dab in the middle.

Interested, she walked around the desk to see the plaque right side up. Her heart almost stopped when she read what the engraved portion of the plaque said, and the date.

Grant had been awarded this Employee of the Year plaque just today!

Her stomach dropped. Obviously, he'd done well since he returned from Moonlight Cove. Good for him; she didn't begrudge him his success.

But somehow seeing this award drove home all of the reasons he hadn't stayed in Moonlight Cove. All of the things that had kept him alone in the past, avoiding love and commitment. He'd made those choices and had been happy with them. There was a very good chance he'd be perfectly content to be married to his job for the rest of his life.

Not exactly a news flash.

She turned to stare out the window. Maybe coming here had been a mistake. She'd wanted to be strong and fight for her and Grant...but now, all of her doubts and insecurities wanted to take over. Hard habit to break, apparently.

She clenched her hands. No. Coming here hadn't been a mistake. She would not crumble in a heap of insecurity or second-guess herself. Or Grant. Not again. Shoving her chin in the air, she took a bracing breath, prepared to go after what she wanted. And she wanted Grant with everything in her.

A male voice startled her. "Boy, am I glad I caught you."

Whirling around, she pressed a shaking hand to her galloping heart and saw Grant standing in the doorway, dressed in a well-fitting dark blue suit, white dress shirt and red power tie.

"You scared me!" she said breathlessly. He looked absolutely gorgeous, as usual, with the late-afternoon sun shining through the window to light up his eyes like brilliant blue gemstones.

He walked in and stopped on the other side of the desk. "Sorry. Didn't mean to startle you."

"It's okay." She shifted uneasily, stunned by how much she wanted to walk around the desk and throw herself into his arms. "The receptionist out front said you'd left for the day. I...um, was just going to leave you a note." She gestured helplessly to the desk. "But there's no paper..."

"I did leave," he said, moving around the desk so he was standing right next to her.

"So...why are you back?" she asked, her voice higher than normal.

He smiled, his gaze roaming over her. "I got a call from Aunt Rose."

"What did she want?" Molly asked, although she had a feeling she knew. Was it possible Rose didn't keep her promise? Molly unbuttoned her wool coat and flapped the edges just a bit, looking for cooling airflow. Was it hot in here?

"Are you warm?" he asked.

She chuckled. "Just a bit." Roasting, actually, now that Grant was on the scene.

"Let me take your coat," he said, reaching for the lapels. "I want you to be comfortable."

She could only nod as he pulled the coat off her arms and laid the garment over the back of his desk chair.

Finally she got her mouth to form words. "So, what did Rose want?" she repeated.

"She had some very important news for me," he said, reaching out and taking Molly's quivering hand.

"Really?" She couldn't help but wrap her fingers around his warm hand. "Want to tell me about it?"

He pulled her closer, then took her other hand in his. "She wanted to tell me that you were on your way here to tell me something. Something important."

Molly could only nod. She didn't know whether to kiss or strangle Rose for calling Grant.

Leaning in, his breath whispered over Molly's warm cheek. "Any idea what she was talking about?" he asked next to her ear in a low voice.

She closed her eyes. "She didn't tell you?" Molly managed, but her voice came out in a squeak.

His hands moved up to her shoulders. "Nope. Just that you'd come here." He leaned back slightly and looked deep into her eyes. "Care to elaborate?"

"I came here to tell you that...congratulations for winning Employee of the Year."

"Molly," he chastised softly. He knew her too well.

Standing here, with him so close, she couldn't lie or hide the truth any longer. She owed herself this chance, owed *them* this chance.

She swallowed and met his steady gaze, finding unexpected strength in the fathomless blue depths. And then she took the most frightening leap she'd ever faced.

"Okay." She took a huge breath. "I still love you."

He froze, then closed his eyes, shaking his head. "I'm surprised to hear that, given what I did."

"You didn't—"

"No, no, don't minimize the crummy choice I made." He stroked her cheek and looked deep into her eyes. "I never should have left you. But

I was so scared and confused…I was in over my head—or thought I was—and I fell back on my work to pull me through."

"And?" she said, sensing he needed to say what he had to say, so she'd let him talk.

"And it was the worst thing I've ever done, and I'm sorry." He laughed under his breath. "I got that huge, ugly award over there—which I've coveted for years, by the way—and it meant nothing, made me feel nothing compared to how you make me feel."

She teared up.

"I was on my way out of Seattle when Aunt Rose called," he said quietly.

Molly's heart lifted in tentative joy. "You were?"

"Yup." He pressed a kiss to her forehead, then whispered against her skin, "I had something very important to say."

"Yes?" she asked, her heart beating about a hundred miles per hour.

Pulling back, he framed her face with his hands. "I love you, Molly Kent, and a million Employee of the Year awards wouldn't be enough to drag me away from you."

Astonishment and joy spread through her like a warm, healing tide. Beaming, she fell into his adoring gaze. "Well, isn't that a coincidence," she said before his mouth claimed hers in a tender kiss.

He kissed his way across her cheek, then kissed both of her eyes before he put his arms around her and pressed her even deeper into his embrace. "It's not a coincidence at all. I prayed to God for answers, and this time, He answered me with a resounding 'yes.'"

"He's a pretty smart guy. After all, He helped me find you your perfect match," she said, wrapping her arms around Grant's waist, never wanting to let him go. And now it looked like she wouldn't have to.

"He did, indeed," Grant said, squeezing her closer as he laid his cheek on her head. "And you found yours, didn't you?"

She tilted her head up and whispered, "You know I did."

"Aunt Rose is going to be ecstatic," Grant said. "Should we call her?"

Molly pulled back and took his hand in hers. "Let's go tell her in person."

"You up for the drive back?"

"As long as you're at the wheel, I'm good."

"Well, then, let's go and spread the happy news," he said with a pull on her hand.

She pulled back. "Wait."

He turned.

"I want you to know I'll move to Seattle if that's what's best for us."

He gave her a gentle smile, then reached out

and stroked her chin. "What's best for me is to be with you. So as long as we're together, I'm good. You okay with that?"

A sense of wonder filtered through her. "How could I not be okay with that? You love me, I love you. That's the best news I've had in forever."

"Then grab your coat, sweetheart. It's time for a road trip to Moonlight Cove."

Molly picked up her jacket, happiness like she'd never known spiraling through her, obliterating all of her doubts. All of her walls. For good.

She'd finally found where she belonged. Right here, with this charming, loving, perfect man. Forever.

Life—and love—didn't get any better, any more splendid, than that.

Epilogue

Holding hands with Grant, Molly let herself into Rose and Benny's house after the Easter church service they'd all attended just an hour earlier. Rose had insisted on serving Easter brunch at her house, and had promised her famous honey-basted ham to all of those invited.

As Molly stepped from the blustery April weather into the warm and cozy living room, the savory smell of roasting ham and cheese potatoes teased her nose. Her stomach growling, she noted that she and Grant were the last to arrive; a few sweet, stolen kisses in Grant's car had made sure of that!

Grant's cousin Kim and her new husband, Seth, were seated on the couch, their hands clasped together, looking like the truly devoted couple they were. They had announced Kim's pregnancy just last week, and the whole family was ecstatic to be welcoming a baby into the family by the end of the year.

Their seven-year-old son, Dylan, was on the floor, playing with Jade, Cleo and Jojo. All the dogs' tails were wagging happily as Dylan rolled a tennis ball around for Jade and Cleo to chase.

Jojo let out a hearty yip and Dylan set her down. She ran after the ball and pounced on it. Jade and Cleo both sat down, looking as if they were puzzled about the eight-pound ball of white fluff who'd waylaid their tennis ball.

Rose was undoubtedly in the kitchen putting the finishing touches on the meal. Neil sat in the recliner next to the couch, talking with Benny, Molly's dad and Grant's dad, who'd come into town for the holiday. The Super Bowl they'd all watched together at Molly's in February was undoubtedly their topic of conversation.

The whole scene warmed Molly's heart, most especially her dad's presence. He'd been visiting often, and was even throwing around the idea of moving to Moonlight Cove and opening his own law firm. Of course, the pretty widow he'd met through Rose probably had something to do with his plans. Molly couldn't be happier about her new relationship with him; he'd definitely changed for the better and had cut back on his work hours to spend more time with his family. Having him back in her life thrilled her to no end.

Especially now, when she and Grant had some of their own happy news to share. Feeling the weight of the gorgeous solitaire diamond ring on her left hand sent excitement and happiness zinging through her, making her feel like the luckiest, most blessed woman on the planet.

In the end, Grant had decided to move to Moonlight Cove. There was a big need in town for people with computer troubleshooting skills, and he'd already leased the space next to Bow Wow Boutique and would be opening up shop in a few weeks.

Thank you, God, for bringing Grant into my life and for guiding me and bestowing upon me the wisdom to see how much I love him.

Suddenly, she couldn't wait another moment to make their announcement. Holding off blurting the news all the way through the service had been hard enough. Actually, waiting until morning to share their joy after Grant had proposed last night on the beach in the moonlight had been challenging. The time had come to declare their love in front of the world. Finally.

Grant helped her off with her coat and hung it up in the hall closet.

When he returned, his mouth pressed into a tender smile, she looked at him, hardly able to believe that just four months ago she'd been alone and sure she'd remain that way forever. Funny how just when she'd thought she had everything figured out, God had stepped in and opened her eyes to other possibilities.

"You ready?" she asked, still knocked senseless by his smile. And everything else about him.

Oh, how she loved this amazing man.

He put his arm around her and squeezed, then pressed a lingering kiss to her lips. "I've never been more ready. I love you."

"And I love you."

Hand in hand, they stepped into the living room.

And into their new future together as man and wife, bound by God. Forever and ever.

* * * * *

Dear Reader,

I am so glad you could join me for another story set in Moonlight Cove. I have such fun writing about this town and its people; maybe I'm a small-town girl at heart, even though I live in the relatively large city of Portland, Oregon.

This story went through many iterations before it became *Mistletoe Matchmaker,* so it is a book that is near and dear to my heart, although I have to admit it did give me some fits during extensive revisions. But the core premise stayed pretty much the same from the beginning—being a dog lover, I wanted to write about a hero and heroine who are brought together by a dog. Once the idea was set, I based Jade on my own standard poodle, also named Jade, so the details about Jade are accurate. Standard poodles are extremely smart (my Jade can unzip backpacks to dig out granola bars!), but also have a goofy side along with an extremely intuitive nature I wanted to highlight. I also grew up with schnauzers who were the inspiration for Peter and Parker, so all of the dogs in this book have special meaning to me.

Also, I am pleased to announce that Phoebe will finally get her own book—and love story—when she meets the handsome new sheriff in town.

Look for book 3 in the Moonlight Cove series, *Her Small Town Sheriff,* coming in May 2012.

As always, I love to hear from readers. Feel free to email me at lissa@lissamanley.com.

Blessings,
Lissa Manley

Questions for Discussion

1. Molly grew up with a father who was emotionally unavailable. Hence Grant's workaholic nature almost kept her from letting him into her heart. Is this is a valid reaction to something that happened so long ago? Why or why not? Should she have been more open to another relationship, despite her experiences?

2. Grant found Molly's helper tendencies disconcerting, yet he freely offered to help both Molly and Neil several times. Discuss why you think Grant sacrificed his work time instead of ignoring others' needs. What does this say about his character? Was he being true to himself by helping, or not?

3. Grant had a hard time dealing with his grief over his mom's death. Besides losing himself in his work, what are some other ways he could have more effectively dealt with his loss? Was he wrong to stave off his grief with work? Why or why not?

4. Grant thought that God didn't listen to his prayers because his mom died instead of recovering. Molly said that just because Grant didn't receive the answer he wanted from God

didn't mean He wasn't listening. Have you ever felt as Grant did? Was Grant's reaction valid? Why or why not?

5. Molly told Grant that God always listened, and answered yes, no or not right now. Discuss your opinion of this statement and its ramifications in your personal commitment to your faith and spirituality.

6. Molly liked being needed but didn't like anyone helping her. Was this a realistic expectation for herself, or do you think everyone needs help now and then, no matter the reason for their independence? What would have been a more realistic expectation on her part?

7. Phoebe told Molly she thought Molly wanted so badly to set Grant up with someone so Grant would be unavailable, but Molly denied this. Was Molly being truthful? If not, was her reaction justifiable considering her background and her desire to avoid romance?

8. Grant agreed to Phoebe's plan for the two of them to go on a date to get Molly to back off trying to fix them up. Given Grant's goal of meeting his deadline, was he wrong to agree to Phoebe's plan? Was he dishonest? Or simply

reacting realistically to the situation, given his desire to not date anyone and the time crunch he was experiencing?

9. Grant seeing Jade behaving in the hospital ward was intended to be a metaphor for his own realization that sometimes people, including him, are not always what they seem on the outside. Have you ever realized something important about life or learned a profound lesson through some seemingly unrelated incident? Discuss.

10. Molly's father realized how wrong he'd been to shut Molly out when someone in his law firm died and no one came to the funeral. Was this a realistic way for him to learn this lesson? If not, what would have been more realistic?

11. Molly's "love language" involved helping others whenever she could. What is your "love language"? Discuss other "love languages" you have encountered in your life, and whether this language actually made you feel loved.

12. Grant hadn't set foot in a church since his mom died, having lost his faith in a God whom he felt hadn't answered his prayers.

Did he overreact, and if so, was his response in any way justified? Do you think he would have been better off to look to God for comfort through prayer and worship? Why or why not?

13. Grant didn't get a lot of respect in high school, fueling his desire for career respect in the story. Was his desire for validation through job success wrongheaded? Understandable? Foolish? If none of these, what was it in your opinion? Discuss some of your wrongheaded actions that have, or have not, worked for you in the past, and how you might have handled the situation differently in hindsight.

14. At the end of the book, Grant realized that once he had the career accolades he wanted so badly, the recognition wasn't as great as he'd thought it would be. Discuss why he had this response, whether his reaction to getting the Employee of the Year award was believable and/or convincing and how his realization precipitated his epiphany about loving Molly.

LARGER-PRINT BOOKS!

GET 2 FREE
LARGER-PRINT NOVELS
PLUS 2 FREE
MYSTERY GIFTS

Love Inspired

Larger-print novels are now available...

YES! Please send me 2 FREE LARGER-PRINT Love Inspired® novels and my 2 FREE mystery gifts (gifts are worth about $10). After receiving them, if I don't wish to receive any more books, I can return the shipping statement marked "cancel". If I don't cancel, I will receive 6 brand-new novels every month and be billed just $4.99 per book in the U.S. or $5.49 per book in Canada. That's a saving of at least 23% off the cover price. It's quite a bargain! Shipping and handling is just 50¢ per book in the U.S. and 75¢ per book in Canada.* I understand that accepting the 2 free books and gifts places me under no obligation to buy anything. I can always return a shipment and cancel at any time. Even if I never buy another book, the two free books and gifts are mine to keep forever.

122/322 IDN FEG3

Name _____ (PLEASE PRINT)

Address _____ Apt. # _____

City _____ State/Prov. _____ Zip/Postal Code _____

Signature (if under 18, a parent or guardian must sign)

Mail to the **Reader Service:**
IN U.S.A.: P.O. Box 1867, Buffalo, NY 14240-1867
IN CANADA: P.O. Box 609, Fort Erie, Ontario L2A 5X3

Not valid to current subscribers to Love Inspired Larger-Print books.

**Are you a current subscriber to Love Inspired books
and want to receive the larger-print edition?
Call 1-800-873-8635 or visit www.ReaderService.com.**

* Terms and prices subject to change without notice. Prices do not include applicable taxes. Sales tax applicable in N.Y. Canadian residents will be charged applicable taxes. Offer not valid in Quebec. This offer is limited to one order per household. All orders subject to credit approval. Credit or debit balances in a customer's account(s) may be offset by any other outstanding balance owed by or to the customer. Please allow 4 to 6 weeks for delivery. Offer available while quantities last.

Your Privacy—The Reader Service is committed to protecting your privacy. Our Privacy Policy is available online at www.ReaderService.com or upon request from the Reader Service.

We make a portion of our mailing list available to reputable third parties that offer products we believe may interest you. If you prefer that we not exchange your name with third parties, or if you wish to clarify or modify your communication preferences, please visit us at www.ReaderService.com/consumerschoice or write to us at Reader Service Preference Service, P.O. Box 9062, Buffalo, NY 14269. Include your complete name and address.

LILPI1B

SUSPENSE

RIVETING INSPIRATIONAL ROMANCE

Watch for our series of edge-
of-your-seat suspense novels.
These contemporary tales
of intrigue and romance
feature Christian characters
facing challenges to their faith...
and their lives!

AVAILABLE IN REGULAR
& LARGER-PRINT FORMATS

For exciting stories that reflect traditional values,
visit:
www.ReaderService.com

LISUSDIR11B

Reader Service.com

You can now manage your account online!

- Review your order history
- Manage your payments
- Update your address

We've redesigned the Reader Service website just for you.

Now you can:

- Read excerpts
- Respond to mailings and special monthly offers
- Learn about new series available to you

Visit us today:
www.ReaderService.com

RS10